GRAND SLAM

RITCHIE PERRY

Pantheon Books, New York

LIBRARY OF CONGRESS CATALOGING IN PUBLICATION DATA

Perry, Ritchie, 1942–
    Grand slam.

    I. Title.
PZ4.P4646Gr 1980   [PR6066.E72]   823'.914   80-7722
ISBN 0-394-51271-5

Manufactured in the United States of America

FIRST AMERICAN EDITION

PROLOGUE

'It certainly is a lovely view,' Vanessa agreed.

She was by the french windows in the living-room. From where she was standing she could look out across the lawns and flowerbeds of the carefully tended garden. On the far side the branches of the two copper beeches acted as a frame for the rectangular tower of the village church almost a quarter of a mile away across the fields.

'I'm glad you like it,' Alistair responded, bending down to kiss her neck. 'I want your stay here to be a very happy one.'

Oh Christ, Vanessa thought disgustedly, what on earth am I doing here? Unfortunately, she already knew the answer to her question. She realized what was expected of her before she'd agreed to come but she hadn't met Alastair at the time. He even talked like a character straight from the pages of a woman's magazine.

'Do you want to see the rest of the house?' he asked.

He was standing behind her, pressing himself against her buttocks. As he spoke, he'd moved his hands up from her waist to cup the underside of her breasts.

'I'd like that.'

She only wished she liked his gentlemanly mauling and heavy breathing. Or that she could have found some facet of him, however small, which might have sparked a physical response of her own. Although she hadn't relished the prospect when David had first asked her, she'd allowed herself to be persuaded. His persuasiveness was one of the things which made him so bloody dangerous. In his presence it was almost as though she had no mind of her own. It's high time I stopped drifting, Vanessa told herself firmly, and started making my own decisions again. She had no doubts at all about what her first one would be.

While Alistair went through the guided-tour routine Van-

5

essa did her best to cut him out of her consciousness, answering his questions automatically. An Oxford education had its limitations, and it certainly hadn't taught her how to cope with a situation like the one she found herself in now. She still wasn't sure how she intended to handle Alistair when they reached the master bedroom.

'This is where we'll be sleeping,' Alistair told her, placing a proprietorial arm around her shoulders.

It should have been Vanessa's cue, the moment when she explained that she couldn't go through with the charade. Unfortunately, she was distracted by the sight of the old-fashioned school uniform which was laid out neatly on the bed.

'Is that for me?'

The incredulity was apparent in her voice.

'I would like you to wear it, yes.'

However hard Vanessa tried to fight it, she could feel the laughter bubbling up. Or perhaps it was hysteria, she couldn't be sure.

'I'm sorry,' she spluttered, tears of laughter forming in her eyes, 'but I can't help it. It's so damned funny.'

'It wasn't intended to be.'

Although she realized the man was deeply offended and she wanted to stop, her laughter had assumed a life of its own. In any case, he probably wouldn't have believed her if she'd tried to explain that most of her mirth was directed at herself. It was as though a set of blinkers had been removed from her eyes. Suddenly she was able to pinpoint all the absurdities of her behaviour over the past few months. She could trace the unbroken sequence of mistakes which had led her to this bedroom where some middle-aged lecher expected her to cavort around in a gym-slip and navy-blue knickers. The whole situation was simply too ridiculous for words. At least Vanessa thought it was, until Alistair slapped her viciously across the face, banging her head against the door-jamb.

'Are you all right?'

Now he'd finished with her Alistair was all sweaty concern, leaning over her where she lay on her back on the bed. The remains of her clothing were scattered about the bedroom, but Vanessa wasn't sure what had happened to the last shreds of her self-respect.

'It wasn't that bad, was it?' Now Alistair was seeking for reassurance, ego and erection subsiding at the same time. 'Let's face it, you quite enjoyed yourself once you stopped struggling.'

Please God, he can't really believe that. The unspoken words were almost a scream inside Vanessa's head. Perhaps she should have gone on fighting until he'd been forced to knock her unconscious. Then there would have been no possible way he could justify what he'd done.

This was what shamed her most, even more than the physical indignity. As Alistair had said, there had come a point when she'd stopped fighting, when she'd given in to the inevitable. God knew, though, she'd done her best to resist until then. She'd scratched and she'd bucked and she'd kicked but it hadn't seemed to make any difference. Her clothes had been on the floor, she'd been on her back on the bed and nothing on earth was going to stop him jamming himself into her. Lie back and enjoy it, wasn't that what they said? Well, she'd lain back in the end, for all the good that it had done her. It could even be, Vanessa thought, that I shan't ever enjoy normal sex again. That really would be a shame, because it had been so good when the partner and circumstances had been right.

'You just stay where you are,' Alistair was saying. 'I'll make you a nice cup of tea.'

He spoke as though this would be the answer to everything, a panacea for what had taken place a few minutes before. As soon as he'd left the bedroom Vanessa forced herself to move, slowly and gingerly easing herself out of the bed. Quite apart from an assortment of bruises she hadn't been ready for him, especially not somebody his size, and she was still hurting. Once in the bathroom she bolted the door and

7

then ran a bath, sitting on the lavatory seat and watching until the water was almost level with the overflow. He came up and banged on the door, shouting something to her, while the bath was still filling, but Vanessa ignored him completely. Although she doubted whether any number of baths would make her feel really clean, at least this one would be a start.

It was over an hour later that Vanessa eventually went downstairs, wearing the tattered remnants of her clothes. Finding David with Alistair in the living-room came as no real surprise. She'd assumed that Alistair would contact him at the earliest opportunity.

'We were beginning to become rather worried about you, Vanessa,' David said.

There was no hint of apology or concern in his voice, and this made it much easier. Although Vanessa looked him straight in the eye, she was pleased to discover there was no reaction at all. It really would have been the limit to go through the scene upstairs only for David to sweet-talk her into acceptance. Her anger was about all she had at the moment, and she wanted to hang on to it.

'Aren't you a little bit late for that?' Vanessa enquired, making no attempt to conceal her bitterness. 'Didn't he tell you what's been happening here?'

'Alistair did say there had been a misunderstanding.'

'Oh, is that how he described it? Maybe I'm a bit prejudiced but I'd have said it was a little more than a misunderstanding.'

'Perhaps I phrased myself badly.'

David's voice was soothing.

'Too right you did. I'll tell you precisely what happened. That pompous bastard beat me up and when he'd finished doing that he raped me.'

'Come now, Vanessa. Aren't you blowing the incident up out of all proportion?'

His determined smile was becoming a trifle ragged.

8

'Like hell I am,' Vanessa retorted. 'I can show you the bruises if you like.'

'Listen, I'm very sorry about what happened but try and look at it from my point of view.' It was the first time Alistair had spoken since Vanessa had come into the room and he sounded nervous. 'Nobody forced you to come here. You knew exactly what the arrangement was supposed to be.'

'It didn't say in the prospectus that forcible rape was an optional extra if I decided to change my mind. Come on, David. Lend me your coat and let's get out of here.'

She didn't speak to Alistair again, or even look at him, before she left the house.

Look on the bright side, Vanessa tried telling herself. Hadn't David told her it was for her own good, and wasn't he supposed to have a hot line direct to the Almighty? It amazed Vanessa to think she'd ever believed all the claptrap. Or, to be more honest, that she'd allowed herself to accept his claims without argument. Come to that, a lot of the things she'd done over the past few months amazed her now she sat down and thought about them. There she was with the kind of IQ which should have made her one of the intellectual elite, yet, after Mum's death, she'd opted out. She'd deliberately put her brain into cold storage and allowed a megalomaniac satyr to dictate her life for her. She didn't even have Mandy's excuse that she was a true believer. She'd been aware of the phoniness, chicanery and speciousness from the very beginning and she'd chosen to shut this awareness out.

If she hadn't been so frightened, Vanessa might have derived some amusement from her own stupidity. Earlier in the day she'd decided that the period of drifting was over, that she'd put her mistakes behind her. And then, immediately afterwards, she'd made the biggest mistake of all. OK, she'd just been raped and she hadn't enjoyed the experience one little bit. It still terrified her to think how easily it had been done, despite her resistance. Even so, there could have been no excuse for her behaviour once they were back at the commune.

'How do you feel now?' David had asked.

Her mistake had been to believe that his evident solicitude was for her. She should have had the sense to realize that David only ever cared for himself.

'Dirty,' she'd answered. 'Used. And very, very angry.'

'I suppose that's only natural after what happened. I should never have asked you to do it for me.'

'There's a lot of things which should never have been done.'

This was when she'd turned on her heels and started up the stairs.

'Where are you going?'

'Upstairs to pack. I'm leaving.'

'But I don't want you to leave, Vanessa, especially in your present mood.'

She'd recognized all the danger signs, this was what Vanessa found hardest to forgive. She'd noticed the change in David's voice. She'd been aware of what he was probably capable of. And yet she'd deliberately applied the spur. Stupid, futile pride had stopped her from backing down, from biding her time until the incident had been forgotten and she could have slipped away unnoticed.

'Quite honestly,' she'd said, 'I don't give a damn what you want any more. I'm going home and that's an end to it.'

It hadn't been, of course. She hadn't even managed to finish packing before Carl and Steven had come for her. Since then she'd been locked in the cellar, cold, hungry, and more frightened than she'd ever been before in her life. Too much had happened to her already for Vanessa to have any illusions about what probably lay ahead.

The three men were alone in the room, seated at the table and drinking coffee. David, by far the oldest and the acknowledged leader, sat at the head of the table. Carl and Steven, who were both in their early twenties, sat on either side of him. None of them was paying any attention to the noise coming from the front of the house where the rest of the group was assembled.

'It's too bad about Vanessa,' David was saying. 'I had great hopes for her.'

'She certainly is a looker,' Carl agreed with an appreciative leer.

David shot him a sharp, hostile glance.

'I didn't mean that. Sex isn't important to me. I just do what I have to to keep them happy.'

The look which passed between the two younger men was distinctly sceptical but neither of them challenged the statement. They weren't about to bite the hand which fed them.

'What I meant,' David continued, 'is that Vanessa is different. She's more intelligent than the others.'

'That's what makes her dangerous.'

'Sure, and she knows some very important people too. If she went to the cops about Brown, the shit really would hit the fan.'

'Wouldn't that be his problem?'

Carl's obtuseness irritated the older man, but he was careful not to allow this to show.

'Listen, as long as we're living in Brown's place, his problems are our problems. Vanessa could blow the whole deal for us. If the newspapers ever get a hold of this, we're going to have to start all over in another country.'

'So we change the way she feels,' Steven suggested. 'We've done it before. She stays in the cellar and we keep working at her until she sees the light.'

There was authority in the way David shook his head.

'We can't take the chance. We already fucked up once in Morocco. If we keep this up, we won't have any place left to go.'

'OK,' Carl said nonchalantly. 'We do the other.'

For a long moment none of the men spoke. Then David broke the silence.

'They can't trace her to us. Nobody knows where she is.'

'Brown knows,' Steven pointed out.

11

'He won't dare say anything. If he does, he'll land himself in trouble.'

'There's no guarantee of that. Anybody who keeps his brains where he does can't be trusted.'

'Well, you better fix it so he'll keep quiet. Set things up so he'll have to keep his mouth shut.'

David was careful not to ask for any details. He didn't want to know. He looked after the young men well and, in return, they afforded him their specialist skills when the need arose. So far they hadn't let him down.

'How about Mandy?' Steven asked.

'What do you mean?'

The connection wasn't immediately obvious to David.

'The two of them came here together. She's Vanessa's only link with Oxford.'

'They're pretty close,' Carl agreed. 'She might react badly if Vanessa disappears.'

There was only a second's hesitation before David spoke.

'You just do what you have to do,' he decided.

The discussion was closed as far as he was concerned. The two younger men waited until he'd left the room before they turned to one another.

'What a waste,' Steven said with a grin. 'A good-looking pair like them.'

'Don't worry, Steve,' Carl answered. 'There's plenty more where they came from. Religion is a wonderful thing.'

They were both laughing as they started across the hall towards the cellar stairs.

CHAPTER I

My cards hadn't changed since I'd last looked at them. After what had gone before there was only one possible bid.

'Seven diamonds,' I said.

Avarice had made my voice husky and I lubricated my throat with a gulp of whisky. I wasn't a bridge fanatic, and the bidding wasn't usually enough to set my pulse racing, but this hand was something special. We'd agreed to play the last rubber for £2 a point, which meant my grand slam was going to be worth £3,000. With another £1,400 thrown in for rubber it was going to be a profitable night, even after I'd deducted my losses to date. For this kind of money I'd have dinner at Pawson's club at any time he cared to invite me.

'Pass,' Winter said.

He was sitting to my left.

'Pass,' Pawson concurred from opposite me.

'Double.'

I sorted through my cards yet again, then sneaked a sideways glance at Ennals. Dun and Bradstreet was only just down the road, and if the agency had been open I'd have liked to rush over and obtain a credit rating for him and his partner. As it was I had to take them on trust. I had to assume that anybody who could afford the club's annual subscription could also afford to drop £12,000 on a single hand of bridge. This was precisely what they both stood to lose after my next bid.

'Redouble,' I said, my voice huskier than ever.

'Sweet Jesus Christ!' Winter didn't sound as though he was enjoying himself. 'I hope you know what you're doing, Arthur.'

Ennals forgot whatever he might have said in reply when Pawson withered him with a glance. Until this stage it had been quite a sociable game, with nobody worrying too much about the odd comment during play. Now there was so much at stake this had all changed.

'It's your lead,' I said to Winter.

'I know,' he muttered.

He was a nervous card player at the best of times, and he'd been perspiring gently all night. Over the last minute or so he'd worked up such a sweat that the collar of his dress shirt was beginning to wilt. Although he didn't say as much, I knew he would have been far happier if his partner had made some other bid apart from doubling me. In that case he might have had some idea what to lead. After two or three false starts Winter eventually came up with a small club. He wasn't to know that his soul-searching had been so much wasted effort. My hand was absolutely solid.

At least, this was what I thought, until Pawson displayed what he had for me in dummy. Then I was working up a sweat of my own which made everything go limp all the way down to my socks. The ace of clubs that Pawson had advertised was there. So were the three diamonds, the queen, and one of the two kings he'd promised me, but of the king of diamonds there wasn't a sign. Even when I re-sorted the dummy I didn't find it stuck behind one of the other cards.

'Is that what you wanted, Philis?' Pawson enquired cheerfully, blithely unaware of my murderous thoughts.

'Sure,' I grunted.

It was no good telling him that he'd buggered up the bidding when I'd asked him for kings. What I had to do, if only for the sake of my bank balance, was make the best of a bad job. It was no longer a formality, but the grand slam was still there, despite Pawson's efforts to bankrupt me. Although I couldn't think why he'd decided to advertise it, the missing king had to be with Ennals on my right, probably together with the other two small diamonds which were missing. If it wasn't I was sunk.

I took the first trick in dummy with the ace of clubs, discarding a heart from my own hand, then led a small diamond through Ennals. Although I didn't like the confident way he played low himself, I was committed by now, and threw down the queen of diamonds. If nothing else I made Winter happy. He was smiling all over his face when he took the trick with the missing king.

'Shit,' I said in a loud voice.

Several heads turned at nearby tables, but I didn't give a damn. Instead of winning myself a small fortune I'd just dropped £800.

Three-quarters of an hour later Pawson and I had lost the rubber as well and I'd signed a cheque for a little more than two thousand pounds. It was one of those occasions when I wished I kept a pet. Then at least I'd have had something to kick.

'Don't brood about it, Philis,' Pawson said, standing beside me at the top of the steps while we waited for his car to be brought round. 'I'll cover your losses.'

'Like hell you will,' I growled.

The last thing I needed at that moment was a dose of his condescension.

'It's only reasonable,' Pawson pointed out. 'I can afford it, and it was my mistake which cost us the slam.'

'That's as may be, but I knew who my partner would be when I agreed to play. In any case, I wouldn't have been offering you any of my winnings if we'd been lucky.'

When Pawson turned his head away I assumed he was looking to see whether his car was on its way. It was only later that I realized he must have been crippling himself with laughter. Although I'd no way of knowing this at the time, Pawson was playing God again, and I was the ball of clay he'd chosen to practise with.

CHAPTER II

'What's it like to be poor?' Amanda enquired.

She was sitting on the corner of my desk, idly swinging one shapely leg. If it hadn't been shapely it wouldn't have matched the rest of her.

'Terrific,' I told her. 'It's always been my ambition to be a pauper.'

'Don't let it get you down, Philis.' Her cheerful smile showed how well she herself was weathering my misfortune. Like everybody else in the department she found it a big joke. 'My feelings about you haven't changed, even if you are poor. You're still the most exciting man who's never come into my life.'

There were odd occasions when I caught myself wondering why I hadn't. Amanda was attractive and pneumatic and available, three of the qualities I normally admired in a woman. Perhaps I was growing old. Or, more likely, perhaps maturity had taught me to be prudent. Since Lunt had established his Psychological Evaluation Unit I'd done my best to avoid any involvement with the department's female staff. Whatever Lunt or Pawson might think, I didn't consider my sex life a suitable subject for analysis.

'Did you read the note from Fennel?' Amanda asked.

'I did. I've filed it for future reference.'

Amanda glanced at the wastepaper basket and laughed.

'He did say it was important when he gave it to me.'

'That's nothing new. Anyway, I'm not in the mood for his monthly moan at the moment.'

Fennel worked in Accounts and gave the impression that it was his own money which kept the department running. Every month without fail he dragged me into a running battle over my claims for expenses. This was a complete waste of time for both of us since Pawson was the final arbiter and he always came down on my side unless my demands were too outrageous.

'It can't be anything to do with your expenses,' Amanda told me. 'I was there when they were processed. Fennel made one or two snide cracks about your vivid imagination but he signed them all.'

'So what is it then?'

'I'm not sure. Fennel doesn't take me into his confidence.'

'But?'

'Well, he did pull your file from Personnel. I think it was something to do with holidays.'

'Holidays?' I said sourly. 'What are they?'

All the same, I bowed to the inevitable and took the lift to Accounts. Fennel emphasized the urgency of his summons by allowing me to cool my heels for a quarter of an hour before he was ready to see me. I retaliated by lighting a Senior Service as soon as I was inside his sanctum. Fennel was trying to kick a forty a day habit and finding it hard going.

'Do you have to blow smoke in my face, Philis?' he demanded irritably.

'I'm terribly sorry,' I said, 'but you should try and make allowances for us weak-willed addicts.'

Fennel grunted and started sorting through the papers on his desk.

'It's about your annual leave,' he told me once he'd found what he was looking for. 'There appear to have been some irregularities over the past few years.'

'I know. I've been working unpaid overtime.'

'I wouldn't say it was exactly unpaid, Philis,' Fennel corrected me with a wispy smile. 'Don't forget I enjoy the doubtful privilege of authorizing your expenses.'

As Fennel seemed inordinately pleased with his little quip, I showed my own appreciation with a sneer. I felt he deserved some kind of encouragement. Before he knew it, Fennel might actually develop a sense of humour.

'OK,' I conceded. 'If it makes you any happier, I'll

rephrase what I said. Every year I make arrangements for my holidays and every year something crops up to prevent me going.'

'How very sad.' Perhaps I was doing him an injustice but Fennel didn't appear to have been particularly upset by my tale of woe. 'Unfortunately, the fact remains that your contract says you're entitled to four weeks' paid leave every year. At the moment SR(2) is in breach of this contract. Unless it's sorted out we're likely to have the unions on our back.'

The reference made me smile. Although organized labour hadn't made a great deal of headway in the world of espionage, I was a member of one of the Civil Service white-collar unions. I figured as a field researcher or some other equally unlikely fiction.

'How much time am I owed?' I enquired.

'I make it ten weeks, give or take a few days.'

'That's what I made it. Mr Pawson may not have mentioned it to you but we've reached a gentleman's agreement. When I've accumulated three months I'm taking it in one lump.'

Fennel had begun to shake his head before I'd finished speaking.

'I'm afraid it doesn't work like that, Philis. It's specified as an annual leave. You're not allowed to hoard it.'

'Sort it out with Pawson,' I suggested. 'It's his fault the situation developed.'

Although Fennel always managed to grate on my nerves, this was one occasion when I was determined not to allow him to get me down.

'I'm not trying to apportion blame. All I'm saying is that the situation has to be rectified as soon as possible. You're not operational at the moment, so I've made arrangements for you to commence your leave on the first of next month.'

So much for determination. I took a long, hard look through the window at the snow on the rooftops. The bitter January weather might be a bonus for any resident brass monkeys, but I was allergic to frost-bite.

'You'd better start unarranging then,' I said. 'February and March don't happen to be my favourite holiday months. I prefer a tan to goose-pimples.'

'Why not go abroad, Philis? Follow the sun. It's out of season, so the prices should be pretty reasonable.'

'Reasonable isn't good enough. At the moment I'd be hard pushed to finance a long weekend with the Salvation Army.'

A shrug of the shoulders was Fennel's way of letting me know how much he sympathized with my predicament.

'Your extravagance isn't my concern, Philis, except when it figures on an expense claim. Your leave commences on the first of February, and that's an end to it.'

I didn't leave the matter there, of course, but Fennel was totally impervious to all my arguments. There was an obvious relish in the way he stuck to his guns.

'OK,' I said at last. 'I'll sort it out with Pawson.'

'You can try, Philis, you can try.' Fennel was complacent now, leaning back in his chair with his thumbs hooked into his waistcoat. 'Despite what you evidently think, I'm not attempting to victimize you. I'm merely applying a general directive which came down from Whitehall. You can read the memo if you like.'

This did have the effect of calming me down slightly. Not a lot, mind you, but I was no longer quite so tempted to haul Fennel across his desk and start stamping on him.

'How many other people in the department are affected?' I asked suspiciously.

'None,' Fennel answered, more complacent than ever. 'Have a nice holiday.'

It was late afternoon before Pawson was free to see me. By then word had passed around, and everybody in the building was doing their best to avoid me. Peter Collins did stick his head round the door to enquire if I fancied making up a four at bridge, but he only tried this the once. The dent in the woodwork was visible proof of how close I'd been to hitting him with the ashtray.

Taken separately the two incidents wouldn't have bothered me too much. Although I never enjoyed losing money, especially in large amounts and as the result of somebody else's mistake, I wouldn't have gambled at all if I hadn't been prepared to accept a loss. Nor did I have any rooted aversion to holidays. I enjoyed them as much as the next man, and under normal circumstances I'd have been delighted to be given ten weeks to call my own regardless of the time of year. The only fly in the ointment was that I had expensive tastes. To get the best out of a break from work I needed money, and this was precisely what I didn't have since the previous night.

Given time, and provided I slightly bent one or two of the departmental rules, I knew precisely how I could recoup my losses. What I couldn't possibly do was refill my coffers before the beginning of February. This was why I asked for a stay of execution when I eventually saw Pawson. By June, I calculated, I could build up my bank balance to a respectable level again.

'No can do,' Pawson said with a regretful shake of the head. 'I'd like to help since I'm largely to blame, but it's out of my hands. Any backlogs of leave have to be cleared before the start of the new financial year. That only gives us until the beginning of April.'

I said something unprintable and lit myself a cigarette. I'd had plans for my holiday and these plans had entailed money. Pawson must have read my thoughts.

'You were intending to go to the States, weren't you?'

'That was the general idea. It seems I'll have to think again now.'

'Come now, Philis. It can't be as bad as that. Since Freddie Laker stirred things up an Atlantic crossing isn't much more expensive than a trip to the Continent.'

'It's not the air fare that bothers me. It's having enough to live on once I reach New York. Last night was only the final straw. Don't forget I'm still paying for my car.'

'Ah yes,' Pawson said. 'Philis's folly.'

He was being unfair. The '76 Jensen convertible had been a real bargain at eleven thousand and it had been my Christmas gesture of appreciation to myself. Two days after I'd taken possession a sweet little old lady had driven into the Jensen while it had been minding its own business, parked outside my flat. Since then it had been in a local bodywork shop for extensive surgery and I'd been using a car from the pool.

'You're sure you can't arrange a postponement until June?' I asked. 'Some of my investments should have paid off by then.'

I was deliberately vague, operating on the principle that what Pawson didn't know couldn't hurt him. Or lead to any charges against me under the Official Secrets Act.

'I'm sorry, but as I said before a postponement is out of the question.' To give him his due, Pawson did sound genuinely sympathetic. 'One possible solution has occurred to me, though. Exactly how long are you due?'

'Ten weeks, give or take a few days.'

'Good.' Pawson was treating me to one of the warm, friendly smiles I'd learned never to trust. 'In that case I think I do have the answer. How do two or three weeks moon-lighting appeal to you? The job I have in mind should pay well enough for you to be able to enjoy the rest of your holiday in style.'

I didn't share any of the enthusiasm Pawson was trying so hard to generate. His suggestion had been just a little bit too casual, and all the little tumblers were clicking into place. I didn't like the pattern I could see emerging.

'Oh Christ,' I groaned. 'How could I have been so dumb? That game last night was rigged. I'm being railroaded again.'

'What on earth are you talking about, Philis?'

Although Pawson's surprise appeared to be as genuine as his sympathy, I no longer believed in either of them.

'You can forget the play-acting,' I told him. 'This is a script we've been through before. I know it off by heart. You

21

have something lined up for me, something so shitty you know I won't agree to it unless I'm under pressure.'

'I'm afraid your paranoia is showing, Philis. All I'm trying to do is help.'

'Of course you are, Mr Pawson, sir.' When I was angry I piled the sarcasm on with a trowel. 'It's exceptionally generous of you, but I'll manage on my own.'

Pawson shrugged his shoulders and made no effort to stop me when I headed for the door. He knew I wouldn't leave it at that.

'Did it make you feel good?' I asked, the door half open. 'Did you enjoy fixing it so you and your friends could rip me off for a couple of thousand pounds?'

There was only the briefest of hesitations before Pawson nodded his head.

'Yes, Philis,' he said. 'I suppose I did. You see, I happen to know where most of your savings came from. I normally turn a blind eye to your little fiddles but I'm not going to have any conscience about skinning you for a few pounds. You could say the money wasn't rightfully yours in the first place.'

It was game, set and match to Pawson and there was nothing left for me to say.

CHAPTER III

There were occasions when I suspected that Pawson might know me a hell of a sight better than I knew myself. It was an invasion of privacy I'd always resent, especially when he steered me along paths I didn't want to follow. The particular path I was steering along on the first of February was the A6, and my destination was just outside Harpenden. As Pawson had known, my anger wasn't self-sustaining. It needed fuel to feed on, and he'd been careful not to provide me with any. Although I still bristled every time I remembered how Pawson and his gentlemanly friends had ripped me off, there was no percentage in living in the past. If I wanted some pocket-money for my trip to the States, I'd have to earn it. So far I hadn't received any better offers than the one Pawson had made me.

Apart from financial necessity I had another reason for going to Harpenden, and my curiosity was a weapon Pawson had often used against me before. Simon Denny, the man I was going to see, was one of those rare people who had managed to become a legend in his own lifetime. More surprisingly, this was a position he'd attained on his own merits and without the assistance of the media. While he'd never taken inaccessability to the lengths of Howard Hughes, Denny had avoided the public eye wherever possible. He remained a man of mystery, and a large part of his fascination was that he'd never been brought into proper focus. As a frustrated journalist had once written, 'Simon Denny remains as elusive as a mirage in the deserts which made him his fortune.' This same journalist had estimated Denny's personal fortune to be in excess of five hundred million pounds. It seemed a hell of a lot of money to make from selling sand.

To begin with, though, Denny hadn't even had any sand to sell. Nor had he appeared to have the potential to become one of the richest men in the world. Palaeontologists weren't normally associated with great wealth, and this was what Denny had once been. By all accounts he hadn't even been a particularly good palaeontologist. Although he participated in one or two archaeological digs prior to the Second World War, no startling discoveries resulted, and he established no real academic reputation. He wasn't a great deal more successful as a soldier, either. Far from being a reincarnation of Lawrence of Arabia he only progressed to the rank of corporal after six years' soldiering.

However, it was in Arabia that he made his fortune. By the early 1950s Denny had managed to scrape together sufficient financial backing to promote his own expedition to the Persian Gulf. Although this expedition was a complete failure in an archaeological sense, it proved to be the making of Denny himself. During the four years he was out there Denny became a very close friend of one of the sons of Said Ibn Taymur, the Sultan of Oman. When the rest of the expedition returned to England Denny was invited to stay on, and this was the turning point of his life.

At the time Oman had been little more than a backwater. The sultan had believed in keeping himself to himself, maintaining diplomatic ties only with the UK, the States and India, and nothing at all had been done to turn Oman into a modern state. More significantly, while oil was being discovered in vast quantities all over the Arabian peninsula, Oman missed out completely. This was probably why the sultan didn't consider himself as being particularly generous when he granted his son's friend the oil concession to a patch of sand in one of the remoter areas of an already remote country.

In fiction, a great reservoir of oil would have been discovered beneath the concession, and Denny would have become a millionaire overnight. However, this was no fairy story, and what Denny did was much, much cleverer. Oil was being discovered all around, the geologists suspected there must be more in Oman itself. This was a belief Denny had been happy to encourage. He formed a company and sold shares in his concession to any of the big oil companies who were interested, which was most of them. Then, in 1964, oil had been discovered in Oman. There wasn't much of it, and none of this oil was anywhere near Denny's concession, but this didn't worry him. He had his first couple of million in the bank, and he'd already moved on.

This was when Denny had stopped being a palaeontologist and had become an entrepreneur. His experiences in Oman had given him both contacts and expertise. It was the kind of expertise which was in great demand all over the Middle East because there were plenty of other countries with a lot of sand to sell. By the mid-1960s Denny had a substantial interest in concessions in Kuwait, the Trucial States, and

Saudi Arabia, which comprised a total area of over 100,000 square miles. He even had the foresight to take out options in the Gulf itself. The beauty of Denny's operation was that he didn't really give a damn whether oil was discovered or not. What he sold the multinationals was the right to look, and his money was in the bank regardless. If oil was discovered Denny earned a 5% royalty on every barrel which was produced. Short of minting your own money I couldn't think of an easier way to make a fortune.

Apparently Denny hadn't been content with his holdings in the Middle East. The grounds surrounding his house were extensive enough to have provided a site for London's third airport, and the building itself must have covered almost an acre. It looked as though it had started off as a manor house back in the seventeenth century and successive owners had simply added pieces here and there as the need arose. While the end product lacked the architectural homogeneity to attract a purist, it was far from unpleasant, and sheer size alone made it impressive. I was glad Denny had to pay the rates, and not me. All I wished was that I'd been able to afford them.

It was something of a disappointment to discover there was no butler. However, a Filipino houseboy was better than nothing, and he was suitably servile. He must have managed to call me 'Sir' at least a dozen times on our lengthy hike along the corridors. The study to which he conducted me was obviously the nerve-centre of the house, complete with Telex and computer terminal. Nevertheless these, together with the battery of telephones on the desk, were the only real concession to the twentieth century. One wall was decorated from floor to ceiling with first editions, unless Denny had cheated and purchased a job lot from a firm of interior decorators. Another displayed a portrait and two engravings which could only have been done by Dürer, while a third featured Denny's collection of antique weapons. I didn't have time to examine them closely, but it seemed as though Denny must have grabbed all of the Archduke Ferdinand's

25

collection which hadn't ended up in the Waffensammlung in Vienna.

Despite the care he'd taken with the setting the only thing Denny had in common with the furnishings was that he was old. No possible stretch of the imagination could describe him as handsome. Going down from the top was an untidy thatch of white hair, rheumy eyes partly concealed behind rimless glasses, heavily-veined nose and bloodhound jowls framing a mouth which was firmly tugged down at either corner. I'd met a lot of people with faces which looked as though they'd been well lived in. Denny's looked as though it had been well slept in as well. However, when he spoke there was nothing old about his voice. There was a resonance to it which added another six inches to his five and a half foot frame.

'It was good of you to come, Mr Philis,' he said. 'Will you have a drink after your journey?'

By the time we'd finished shaking hands I'd mumbled my own few polite words of greeting and settled on a whisky. Although it wasn't a brand I recognized, the whisky tasted like liquid velvet, and I sipped it while I looked at Denny across the fireplace. It was his house, and his problem, so I was leaving the initiative to him.

'How much did Mr Pawson tell you?' he enquired.

'Not a great deal, I'm afraid. All I know is that you have a problem of some description. If I think I can help, and if your proposition interests me, I'm authorized to assist you in my private capacity.'

Denny nodded, setting his jowls in motion.

'That's the way I understand the arrangement, too.'

'However,' I continued, 'perhaps you'd like to satisfy my curiosity before you get down to any details. Precisely how well do you know Mr Pawson? That was something he didn't explain.'

Although I was intrigued to know why Pawson had been so eager to sub-contract my services, there was more than simple curiosity behind my question. It could be important to establish my exact terms of reference.

'We've known each other off and on for almost twenty years,' Denny told me. 'I'm close enough to him to have a pretty shrewd idea of who and what you are.'

'That wasn't quite what I meant. Why should Mr Pawson be interested in doing you any favours? He doesn't normally encourage his employees to seek private employment.'

'I suppose you could call it quid pro quo.' Denny was demonstrating the advantages of a classical education. 'The Middle East has always been a sensitive area and I happen to have the ear of a lot of influential people out there. I've had occasion to be of some considerable assistance to your Mr Pawson in the past.'

I'd suspected it had to be something like this. Pawson didn't believe in gratuitous favours.

'OK, Mr Denny,' I said. 'That seems reasonable enough. All I need to know now is why you wanted to see me.'

There was a momentary pause while Denny deliberated how best to phrase his dilemma. In the end he settled for the blunt approach, shorn of any unnecessary adornment.

'I've lost my daughter,' he told me.

Apart from telling him how careless he must be there wasn't much I could say, so I took another sip of whisky. Denny seemed perfectly capable of filling in the detail without any help from me.

'If I'm honest with myself, I don't suppose I've ever been a particularly good father to Vanessa,' Denny said. 'All too often I've tended to put business ahead of family. My work has meant I'm always travelling. Even when I was at home, business kept on intruding. I work a sixteen-hour day, and until recently I considered this to be a virtue. I never really stopped to consider what I was missing in a family sense. I provided the money and the good things in life, and I left it to my wife to provide the affection and the discipline. It's only in the past few months that I've discovered how mistaken I'd been. I suddenly realized that I didn't know Vanessa at all. I

27

had less idea of what made my own daughter tick than I did of my business associates and competitors. As you can imagine, this came as a rather disturbing insight.'

'They say it's fairly common.' I deliberately kept my tone noncommittal. 'And with all due respect, Mr Denny, I didn't come here for you to bare your conscience to me.'

For an instant naked hostility flared in Denny's eyes. Then he caught himself and managed a wry smile.

'You must excuse me, Philis. I hadn't intended to weep on your shoulder. It's just that you're the first person I've had an opportunity to discuss this with for a long time.'

'Don't you talk about it with your wife?'

I was surprised.

'My wife died almost a year ago, Mr Philis.'

Suddenly I was feeling ashamed of my lack of tact and discernment. I'd read Denny wrong. I'd interpreted his reserve and control as dissociation. It wasn't until he'd mentioned his wife's death that the hurt had really shown through. Now I knew he wasn't simply seeking a salve for his conscience. Denny really did care.

'I didn't know that. I apologize for my earlier remark.'

'Never apologize when you're in the right,' he said. 'That was one of the very first lessons I learned. Anyway, to go back to what I was saying, it was only when my wife became ill that I realized how far Vanessa had grown away from me. Ellen, that's my wife, had what is politely referred to as a nervous breakdown about six months before her death. There was no prior warning. It was as though there had been a total power cut in one section of her brain. She began sentences and never finished them. She forgot the names of close friends, people she'd known for years. And that was only the beginning. As time went on, Ellen became worse. Much, much worse, and to cut a long story short, she eventually had to be institutionalized. All the doctors and psychiatrists agreed that this was the only course, but I wish now that I'd kept her at home with a private nursing staff. She still had coherent patches when she was fully aware of her environment. I suspect it was during one of these periods that she committed suicide.'

Denny had ground to a temporary halt. Although he'd managed to keep most of the pain out of his voice, the emotional build-up had been too much for him. There might even have been a tear or two in his eyes. He tried to conceal how he felt by turning his back on me while he refilled his glass, and I did nothing to disrupt his mood. It would be nice to believe that some day I'd meet a woman who meant as much to me as his wife had evidently meant to Denny. It might have been a year since she'd died, but Denny had been reliving the events leading to her death as though they'd been only yesterday.

'What about Vanessa?' I asked. 'How did she react to her mother's death?'

By now Denny had resumed his seat and appeared to have himself under full control again. He answered my question with an embarrassed shrug.

'I'm ashamed to admit that I don't really know,' he told me. 'She was terribly upset, I know, possibly more upset than I was myself. You might think our grief might have brought us closer together, but it appeared to have the opposite effect. As I've told you, Vanessa and I didn't have any real contact before Ellen's death, and we had even less afterwards. We both withdrew into ourselves. I can't remember either of us explaining to the other how deeply Ellen's death had affected us. I immersed myself in my work, and Vanessa did the same with her studies. Even when we were here at the house together we kept our thoughts to ourselves. We were friendly enough, but without Ellen there was no real bridge between us.'

We were heading back towards the guilty father bit, and this was still territory I wanted to avoid.

'How long ago did your daughter drop out of sight?' I asked.

'It was at the end of October. That makes it three months ago.'

'Three months?' I was unable to keep the surprise out of my voice. 'And you're only just beginning to wonder what might have happened to her?'

'I'm not quite that bad a father, Philis.' Denny's smile was pained. 'Vanessa was gone a fortnight before her college at Oxford wrote to ask whether I knew where she was. As soon as I ascertained that she'd disappeared, I put Abercrombie's on to it. I'd had occasion to employ them in the past, and they're about the best detective agency in the country.'

I nodded my agreement. I'd never had any personal dealings with them but they had the reputation of being a gentleman's Pinkertons.

'What did they turn up?'

'Hardly anything, I regret to say. All they could tell me was that Vanessa had definitely left Oxford of her own free will. She'd gone to considerable trouble to hide her movements.'

'You mean Abercrombie's couldn't locate her?'

Now I really was surprised.

'They spent two whole months on the case and they didn't come up with one substantial lead. In the end Robinson, the person in charge of the investigation, told me I was throwing money down the drain. There was absolutely nothing to suggest any harm had come to her, and the consensus of opinion at Abercrombie's was that Vanessa would surface when she was good and ready. They couldn't hold out any real hope of finding her if she didn't want to be found. She'd made too good a job of covering her tracks.'

Although I wasn't sharing any of my doubts with Denny, and there was insufficient evidence for me to be leaping to any conclusions, I didn't find Abercrombie's interpretation particularly convincing. And I suspected that Pawson must have felt the same. Although I didn't know Robinson it was safe to assume that he was reasonably competent, otherwise the detective agency wouldn't have employed him. If he was, I couldn't believe that Vanessa had managed to vanish into thin air on her own. This should be beyond the capabilities of any student, Oxford education or not. All the signs were that young Miss Denny must have had professional assistance.

There wasn't a great deal more Denny could tell me about his daughter. She'd gone, nobody knew where, and that was that. However, he did give me some background material, a kind of character reference for a daughter he wished he'd known better.

According to the authorized version, Vanessa was intelligent, sensitive and had a well-developed sense of humour. She was also inclined to be secretive, which was why I wasn't necessarily placing a great deal of faith in what Denny had to say. My own sex life had consisted of a long succession of relationships with daughters, so I had a pretty fair idea of how well the average parents understood their offspring. I guessed that a copy of Robinson's report on his abortive investigation might prove far more valuable, originating as it did from an unprejudiced source. Nevertheless, there were other aspects which only Denny could clarify for me.

'Why me?' I enquired. 'Investigative work isn't exactly my forte. I'm more of a blunt instrument.'

'Abercrombie's specialize in private investigations,' Denny pointed out, 'and they didn't come up with a thing. I'm hoping a slightly different approach may pay dividends. Besides, I'm not sure that you aren't underestimating yourself. Mr Pawson did mention that intuition was one of your major talents.'

'Sure. I'll simply gaze into my crystal ball and Vanessa will be as good as found.'

'I know it won't be easy. You can only do your best.'

He was fencing with me, deliberately avoiding an obvious possibility. I couldn't decide whether Denny was trying to cultivate a blind spot or whether he was frightened he might scare me off.

'Mr Denny,' I said carefully, 'you're not a fool and neither am I. We're not likely to make much progress unless we're honest with one another. I think I know why Mr Pawson was so eager to push me in your direction. Do you?'

There was only the briefest of hesitations before Denny nodded.

'It wasn't something we discussed, but I can make a very shrewd guess at what he was thinking.'

'Good. And was this a thought which had already occurred to you?'

Now it was Denny's turn to choose his words carefully.

'It was one of a number of possibilities I considered. I move in somewhat sensitive areas, and I also happen to be wealthy. A kidnapping could make sense either from a political or economic standpoint.'

'But there has been no ransom demand.'

'Precisely.'

Denny spoke as though this meant we could dismiss any thoughts of kidnapping, but I wasn't prepared to leave the matter there. I knew Pawson would never have gone to so much trouble to soften me up unless he'd considered there was a strong likelihood of the department becoming involved at some stage. As he hadn't had sufficient grounds to initiate an official enquiry, he'd pitchforked me into a situation where Denny would be picking up the tab. Meanwhile, the department would be handily placed to intervene when and if this became necessary.

'Providing you're holding a hostage who is valued,' I explained, 'the timing of the ransom demand becomes a matter of choice. Some of the terrorist organizations are becoming quite sophisticated nowadays. When they plan an operation they try to allow for every possible contingency. It could be that Vanessa is being held in reserve as some kind of ace in the hole.'

Denny was actually smiling at me as he shook his head.

'I'd be a fool to deny the possibility, but I think what you're suggesting is a trifle far-fetched. Everything I've learned so far indicates that Vanessa left Oxford voluntarily. I've never heard of a kidnap victim clearing out her current account on her way into captivity.'

32

I had, but I didn't argue with him. I simply hoped my suggestion really was as far-fetched as Denny had found it.

'Will you try to find Vanessa for me?'

I'd run out of questions and Denny evidently considered it to be his turn. The clearly detectable anxiety in his voice was a pleasant sop to my ego. I'd no idea what Pawson had said to sell me to the entrepreneur, but it must have been quite convincing. Come to that, he'd done quite a job on convincing me. I hated unsolved mysteries.

'OK,' I said. 'I'll do my best, but don't expect any miracles. Let's say that I'm at your disposal for a fortnight. I should know by then whether or not I'm wasting my time.'

'That sounds very reasonable. Precisely how much are your services going to cost me?'

This was a question which had been bothering me all the way to Harpenden. I'd failed to come up with a satisfactory answer.

'I'm not really sure,' I admitted. 'I don't know the going rate for this kind of work.'

'Abercrombie's were charging me a hundred a day plus expenses,' Denny told me. 'That seemed fair.'

If he was talking about pounds, and not pence, I could only agree with him. It made me wonder why I risked my life for the pittance SR(2) paid me. And why I'd put a time limit on how long I'd be working for Denny.

'I don't work Sundays,' I decided after a moment's reflection, 'and there won't be any beautifully typed report at the end of the fortnight. Call it a level thousand plus incidental expenses.'

Although I was rather disappointed that Denny didn't press me to accept more, I did receive some consolation from his next words.

'Is half in advance all right by you?' he enquired.

While he filled out the cheque I tried to remember the last occasion I'd turned down an offer of five hundred pounds. Once I had it safely tucked away in my wallet, along with the unpaid bills, Denny and I didn't have a great deal more to say to one another apart from exchanging a few polite farewells. In the process I contrived to drink another glass of Denny's whisky. It was one of the best adverts for private enterprise that I'd had the privilege to come across.

CHAPTER IV

When I left Denny I already knew what my first step would be. After I'd telephoned Abercrombie's the following morning I changed my mind. Robinson was appearing in court in connection with another investigation and would be tied up for at least a couple of days. In view of what Denny was paying me I could hardly justify sitting around and twiddling my thumbs for the next forty-eight hours.

Fortunately, there was an alternative starting point, which was why I was on the M40 before lunchtime, driving towards Oxford. I'd spent most of the previous night ploughing through Robinson's written report, and the ground he'd covered had seemed depressingly comprehensive. In theory it was impossible for anybody to go missing nowadays, and the man from Abercrombie's had followed up all the obvious lines of enquiry. Apart from all the governmental computers and agencies which kept tabs on the country's citizenry, he'd tried several long shots like the major airlines. He'd even gone so far as to check with Interpol to discover whether anybody carrying British passport number such and such in the name of Vanessa Anne Denny had come to their attention in any connection.

The reward for his diligence had been a great fat zero, and his interviews with Vanessa's friends and acquaintances hadn't been a great deal more productive. They'd all been taped and transcribed, and nobody Robinson had spoken to had admitted to knowing the how, the why or the wherefore. I might have found this unanimity suspicious in itself if Robinson hadn't inserted one of his dry footnotes at the end of the transcripts. He stated that in his professional opinion none of the people he'd spoken to had been withholding anything. I was developing a healthy respect for Robinson's expertise, and his professional opinion was good enough for me.

However, there were two aspects of the report which I'd found of special interest. Firstly, there was the number of young men, mostly students, who could be numbered among Vanessa's regular acquaintances. Reading between the lines it wasn't hard to deduce that three or four of them at least had been on intimate terms with her. This discovery had helped to make Vanessa more human for me. I'd never completely bought Denny's description of some Oxford Vestal Virgin, and an insight into her frailties made her easier to understand. It also provided me with a viable alternative to the kidnap theory. Although I hadn't studied the official police statistics, I did know that young women had been running off with young men since time immemorial. Robinson hadn't dug up any hard evidence to suggest this but it was a possibility I'd have to bear in mind.

The second discovery was far more significant. In the course of Robinson's investigations he'd ascertained that Vanessa had changed after her mother's death. None of her friends had satisfactorily managed to put a finger on the exact nature of this transformation, but there was a general consensus; Vanessa's attitudes and behaviour had been different in the months after Mrs Denny's funeral. Most significant of all, Vanessa had made herself a new friend, a girl who had no apparent connection with the university. None of Vanessa's student acquaintances had actually met her, but one of them had come up with a name and Robinson had managed to track her down. At least, he'd tracked down the address where Mandy Collison had used to live before she'd disappeared as thoroughly as Vanessa had done.

This address in Cowley was going to be my first port of call in the Oxford area. In the two months since Abercrombie's had dropped their investigation there had been no news of

Vanessa at all, but this didn't necessarily hold true for her friend Mandy. My first priority was to discover whether or not she'd surfaced, so it was rather frustrating to discover there was nobody at home at the address I'd obtained from Robinson's report. Fortunately, it was the kind of terraced street where everybody knew everybody else's business, and the next-door neighbour was most helpful. Bob and Jenny, alias Mr and Mrs Roberts, alias Mandy's brother-in-law and sister, had gone to Abingdon, and wouldn't return until mid-afternoon. This gave me as good an excuse as I was ever likely to have to invest some of Denny's money in the pub at the end of the road.

It was almost four o'clock before the Roberts family returned. I sat in my car and watched them all pile out of their battered 1100; a pale, washed-out blonde in her mid-thirties, a burly, sullen-looking man who was a few years older, and a couple of squalling brats who would have made a good advertisement for abortion. They couldn't muster a cheerful face between the four of them, and I didn't need to be a mind-reader to guess that the day out hadn't been a success. Nor was Mrs Roberts doing anything to guarantee an improvement now they were home. She didn't stop nag-ging from the moment she left the car until she vanished inside the front door, and she was totally impartial in her tongue-lashing. All the other three received their fair share of abuse, and I thought it might be diplomatic to wait until the family crisis had stabilized before I announced my presence. This was why I was still sitting in my car a couple of minutes later when Mr Roberts came storming out of the house, slam-ming the door behind him.

I watched him until he was out of sight, then took a couple of deep breaths and clambered out of the car. As the Roberts feud gave every indication of turning into a vendetta, I couldn't see that waiting any longer was likely to be of any benefit. By the time I reached the door I was no longer so sure I'd made the right decision. Mrs Roberts's voice was now an hysterical shriek, and the children's feet were pounding up the stairs, hoping to escape before she put any of her threats into practice. Although she didn't accompany them, Mrs Roberts continued to scream words of encouragement to her offspring, employing the kind of language which had never been recommended by Dr Spock. When I rang the doorbell the tirade was abruptly cut short in mid-sentence. I only had to wait a few seconds before the door was opened.

'Mrs Roberts?' I enquired, treating her to a big, friendly smile.

'Yes,' she snapped. 'What do you want?'

'I represent the Beechwood Assurance Company,' I said, deciding friendliness was wasted on her. 'I was hoping to have a few words with you about your sister.'

'You mean Mandy?'

Even as I nodded I knew that somehow or other the interview had turned sour. While Mrs Roberts had a shrew's face to begin with, the mere mention of her sister had been enough to mould her features into lines of uncompromising hostility. She didn't allow me an opportunity to explain where the fictitious insurance company fitted into my scheme of things.

'That's a name we don't mention any more in this house,' she informed me. 'All I can say is good riddance to the cheap little whore.'

These words of familial love had barely finished ringing in my ears before she slammed the door shut. I hiked back to the car, watched by one or two appreciative neighbours, and lit myself a cigarette while I considered the next step. I'd wondered why Robinson had conducted such a brief interview with Mrs Roberts, and now I knew. No help was likely to be forthcoming from her.

Although there was plenty more old ground I could have ploughed over while I was in Oxford, I suspected this would be a waste of my time. Robinson had visited Mandy's friends and workmates, the same way he'd visited Vanessa's, and the result had been the same. All of them had professed to be

37

totally mystified by Mandy's disappearance. Nobody had had any idea why she should want to leave Oxford or where she might go. However, there was one person Robinson had overlooked. So far, nobody had had a chance to talk to Mr Roberts on his own, and it might well be interesting to hear what he had to say. No matter how angry he'd been when he'd come storming out of the house he was bound to return home some time.

I preferred not to wait. If I stayed parked opposite the house Mrs Roberts would undoubtedly be out to see what I wanted, and another encounter with her was the last thing I needed. Fortunately, I'd seen where Roberts had gone. Although the pubs were closed, the Sports and Social Club at the end of the road wasn't, at least, not completely. The steward had remembered to pull down a metal grille over the bar to conform with the local licensing laws, but he'd forgotten the four crates of beer which had been left round the customers' side. Luckily, there was a slate leaning beside them, so that anybody who took advantage of the steward's negligence could chalk up what he'd taken.

There were a dozen or so men in the bar itself, drinking, chatting or playing cards, but Roberts wasn't one of them. I found him on his own in the next room, chasing the balls round the snooker table. When I arrived he was down to the last three reds, and he must have seen Paul Newman or whoever in *The Hustler*. As soon as he became aware of me leaning against the wall he began to introduce a few unforced errors into his game. He wasn't doing much, just enough to change him from a good player into an ordinary one, and I waited confidently for the approach which I knew must come. He did his best to encourage me by making a meal of the pink and black balls, banging them all round the table before he finally put them in the centre pocket.

'Fancy a game?' he asked, leaning on his cue.

'Why not?' I shrugged. 'I don't have anything else to do.'

Roberts grunted and began setting up the table. He didn't

go into phase two until he'd finished with the triangle.

'Do you want to play for love?' he enquired. 'Or would you rather make it more interesting?'

'That all depends on how interesting.'

'Is a quid OK? That shouldn't break you.'

I agreed, if only to put him in the right mood for the questions which would come later. In any case, this was the frame I was supposed to win, and we managed to make it quite a close contest. The only difference between us was that I realized Roberts was playing below par, and he had no idea I was deliberately doing the same.

'Fancy another frame?' Roberts asked once I'd sunk the black.

'Sure.'

'For a fiver this time? We seem to be pretty evenly matched.'

This said a lot about Roberts, that a fiver should be the limit of his ambitions. There was no messing about now. Roberts had begun going for his strokes, and he was considerably better than I'd anticipated. I'd have been hard pushed to beat him even if I hadn't wanted him to win. It was only after Roberts had pocketed his winnings and offered me his commiserations that I told him why I'd visited the club.

'You were looking for me?'

Roberts's surprise was well-larded with suspicion. He inhabited a world where the only people likely to come looking for him were policemen, and debt-collectors.

'You're the only reason I'm here. Come to that, you and your wife are the only reason I came to Oxford.'

Now Roberts could relax. All his problems and villainies were purely parochial.

'Have you seen the wife already?'

I nodded.

'Charming cow, isn't she? Especially when she's in a mood like today.'

'I don't think I did much to improve it. When I mentioned

her sister's name she practically threw me out.'

Roberts found this amusing.

'She would have done. Bringing up Mandy's name is a surefire way of getting into her bad books.'

'So I gathered. There didn't seem to be any love lost between them.'

'You can say that again. Come on. Let's have a drink out of my winnings.'

It took two or three drinks before Roberts explained the bad feeling between Mandy and his wife and, as I'd already guessed, he'd been at the bottom of it. It wasn't a particularly savoury story. Roberts did his best to present it as mutual attraction, regaling me with a wealth of anatomical detail, but it was easy to read between the lines. Tell-tale phrases like 'she played hard to get at first' gave a much better insight into the true nature of the relationship. Roberts had behaved like the oaf he was, pestering his sister-in-law at every opportunity. According to what he told me, Mandy was already selling her body for money.

'I wouldn't have tried it on with her otherwise,' he said. 'Young Mandy was spreading herself about all right.'

'How can you be so sure?'

Robinson's report had given a totally different impression.

'I read her diary, didn't I? She didn't know I had a spare key to the drawer she kept it in. Mandy tried to cover up with some religious mumbo-jumbo when I faced her with it. She fed me some claptrap about doing it for God until I threatened to show the diary to Jenny. I didn't have any more trouble with her after that.'

'Do you still have the diary?'

'No.' Roberts was treating me to an all-boys-together leer which made me want to punch him in the mouth. 'Mandy was desperate to get it back and I allowed her to persuade me. Most enjoyable it was too.'

By now I was finding it next to impossible to form any coherent picture. Unless Mandy had a split personality, either Roberts or Robinson had to be wrong.

'You say Mandy was religious,' I said. 'What exactly do you mean?'

'She was weird. I mean, when she went down on her knees I never knew whether I was due for a prayer or a blow job. She was the same in bed. One minute she was at it like a rattlesnake. The next she was trying to convert me. To be honest, there were times when she was a bloody pain, but she usually made up for it.'

'When did your wife find out what was going on?'

Roberts laughed.

'The same day she kicked Mandy out. That was a nasty moment, I can tell you. I damn near had heart failure when Jenny walked in and caught us. I don't think she could believe her eyes when she saw what we were doing.'

'That's the way it goes.'

Although this wasn't the kind of remark which was designed to earn me an international reputation as a philosopher, Roberts had expected some comment.

'It was a nasty moment, I can tell you,' he reiterated.

'Did you and Mandy keep in touch after she left?'

'No.' Roberts shook his head regretfully. 'I didn't hear a word from her.'

'So you've no idea where she might have gone?'

'Of course I have.' Roberts was looking at me strangely. 'After all, I was the one who had to go down there for the inquest. I'd have gone to the funeral too if Jenny hadn't kicked up such a fuss.'

I suddenly had the feeling that Roberts must have missed out the most important part of his story. Either that or we had our lines crossed.

CHAPTER V

I should have been preparing the little speech I intended to deliver to Denny but I had other, more pressing matters on my mind. The olive-green Marina had been behind me when I reached the M40, and it was still there at the end of the motorway. There was a clearly defined series of responses to a hostile tail, covering a variety of circumstances, but none of them seemed applicable. I couldn't even be sure the tag was hostile, although I did know it was no routine screening. I'd never been important enough to merit day-by-day surveillance by any of the foreign agencies, and the same went for the internal security units. Besides, the man at the wheel of the Marina was making a complete pig's ear of shadowing me. Either he'd left his bifocals at home or he was in dire need of a full refresher course.

Provided it is done sensibly, tagging somebody on a motorway is one of the easiest tails there is. Junctions are usually several miles apart, and it is virtually impossible to detect a tag when he's doing most of the tagging from the front. This was one of the reasons I tried to avoid motorways like the plague when I thought I might be hot. Apparently the joker behind wasn't aware of any of this. He fell into every little trap I set for him, right down to matching his speed with mine. When I slowed, he slowed. When I decided to break the speed limit, he did the same.

His performance was so pathetic that it aroused my curiosity, and I never seriously considered an attempt to ditch him. I could, of course, have done some fancy driving and worked a switch, but I didn't want to risk anything which might upset my tail before I knew more about him. I was especially intrigued to discover why my enquiries about Mandy Collison, deceased, should have earned me this attention. I certainly hadn't done anything else in Oxford to make myself conspicuous. To the best of my knowledge I hadn't even parked on a double yellow line.

As we began to hit the London traffic the Marina moved in closer. This not only enabled me to note the licence number but to see that the driver was a she, not a he. The whole affair was becoming more intriguing by the moment. When I eventually parked outside my flat she drove straight past, the first piece of common sense she'd displayed since we'd left Oxford. However, she didn't go very far. She must have parked just around the corner, because by the time I was upstairs and peeking between the curtains she had installed herself in a shop doorway across the street. She looked as though she might be there to stay, so I took the opportunity to use the telephone. Henderson was on duty, and he was surprised to hear from me.

'I thought you were on holiday, Philis.'

'You thought wrong, then. Holidays are a luxury I can't afford. I want you to track down a registration number for me. It's urgent.'

'You haven't been out talent-spotting again, have you?' Henderson asked suspiciously. 'You're not after the name and address of some sexy looking female you passed on the road?'

'Come now, Alex. Would I abuse the privileges of the department?'

'Of course you bloody well would. As I remember it, it was your bright idea in the first place.'

'OK, OK,' I conceded, 'but this is more or less in the line of duty. And like I said, it's reasonably urgent. Either I've become a cult figure or I have a tag.'

'Do you need help?'

Henderson was suddenly serious again.

'You'd hear me screaming if I did. Are you ready to take down the number?'

Once Henderson had it, he promised to phone back as soon as he had any information. I had time to check the window again and make myself a cup of coffee before he rang.

The vehicle belonged to a car-hire firm in Oxford, unless it had changed owners recently. Henderson had also taken the time to check that the firm was perfectly legal and above board, a piece of courtesy for which I thanked him before I hung up.

What I had to do now was establish contact. Or, to be more precise, make it easy for my new disciple to establish contact with me, because I assumed this was what she wanted. I couldn't think of any other reason why she should be standing out in the street in the kind of weather which kept all sensible people at home in front of their fires.

The girl, and this was all she was, wasn't much better on foot than she had been in the car. Like most novices she tended to work too close, and it was just as well I was determined to make things easy for her. There were a fair number of customers in the King's Arms when I arrived, more than enough to afford her the camouflage she'd want, and I was up at the bar by the time she followed me inside. This gave me the opportunity to observe her in the mirror, and I had to admit that she was a better class of person than the average type who followed me around. Her headscarf and coat concealed most of her to mid-calf, but there was sufficient blonde hair escaping from beneath the scarf, and sufficient contouring to the coat, to suggest that I wouldn't find what was underneath totally displeasing. In any case this didn't matter too much, because her face was clearly visible, and it came very close to being beautiful. Although it didn't have the bone structure to stand the test of time, there was nothing wrong with her nose, eyes or mouth, and her skin tone was good enough not to need any make-up. For the next few years, at least, she wasn't likely to have any shortage of admirers.

She had several inside the King's Arms and she knew it. She might be a failure at shadowing people but she knew all about handling men, and this included picking up strangers in pubs. I'd deliberately stationed myself where there were empty bar-stools on either side of me, and she took the one to my left. She was drinking pineapple juice, and when she'd been served she dug out a cigarette. I didn't exactly fall over with surprise when her lighter refused to work.

'Thanks,' she said once she'd made use of my Ronson. 'My bloody lighter seems to have a mind of its own. I suppose I ought to treat myself to another one.'

I practised a few understanding noises. This was much better than suggesting she should try replacing the flint if she really expected it to work. She'd removed it before coming into the bar.

'I guess it isn't my lucky day.' I'd passed up one opening, but I hadn't turned away, and she was determined to persevere. 'Nothing seems to be going right for me.'

'You have problems?'

Now I was wearing my sympathetic face.

'You could say that, I suppose.' She managed the rueful laugh quite well. 'My boy-friend and I have just had the most godawful row.'

'It happens,' I said. 'The course of true love, and all that.'

If clichés would do there was little point in overtaxing my brain. She responded to my comment with another laugh, allowing her bitterness to show.

'True love doesn't come into it,' she told me. 'Haven't you heard that it's gone out of fashion? My problem is that I walked out on Ray before I remembered I didn't have anywhere else to stay. That's the trouble with having an impulsive nature.'

'It sounds like an exceptionally good argument for a reconciliation.'

I made sure my expression didn't match the words. I didn't want to come on too strong, but I didn't want to make life too difficult for her either.

'No way,' she said. 'When I leave, I leave.'

'In that case let me buy you something a little stronger than pineapple juice. It might not be the answer to anything, but it may give your problems softer edges.'

'No thanks. I don't use alcohol.' She paused long enough

45

to give me an impish smile. She really did have the most kissable lips, and her innocent blue eyes had instant appeal for the dirty old man in me. 'I'd love another fruit juice, though, if that doesn't offend any principles.'

The next half-hour or so passed quite pleasantly without anything significant being said. There was no need for what was happening to be expressed verbally. Caroline had put out the ground-bait. I'd made all the right responses without actually committing myself, and it was simply a matter of her reeling me in when she considered the moment right. After I'd drained my second pint I applied a little pressure of my own.

'Oh well,' I said. 'I suppose I'll have to be off. Will you have another drink on me before I go?'

'You're leaving?'

Caroline wasn't worried. I wasn't exactly rushing off, and she'd noticed how I'd been looking at her since she'd removed her coat.

'I have to,' I explained. 'Another drink and I shan't feel like cooking myself a meal.'

'The joys of a bachelor existence.' Artificial or not, she had a nice laugh. 'Do you live near here?'

'My flat is just around the corner.'

Caroline held back just long enough to make the pause significant.

'I don't suppose it has such a thing as a spare bedroom?'

'I'm afraid not,' I lied, 'but that's no problem. There's plenty of room in mine if you don't mind sharing.'

She didn't, of course, and when I left the pub five minutes later Caroline was on my arm. On the whole I couldn't find too much to fault in her performance in the King's Arms. There was a very thin line between making yourself obvious and being brazen about it, and Caroline had managed to tread it right along the middle.

Working for SR(2) hadn't done a great deal to improve the quality of my sex life. Back in the good old days, before

46

Pawson had bulldozed his way into my life, women had liked me for myself alone. At least, those women of my intimate acquaintance had done. Since I'd joined the department all this had changed. Now I felt a certain sympathy for business tycoons, film stars, and top athletes, because the only difference between them and me was that they had the talent and money.

All too often ulterior motives came between me and my pleasure, and Caroline was a perfect case in point. On the purely physical side, the lovemaking was fine. It was a close encounter of the basic kind and Caroline did more than enough to earn her bed for the night. She was nubile, imaginative and enthusiastic, although she had a markedly sadistic approach which could have done with less of the tooth and nail, and her orgasms may even have been genuine. I might even have cared if I hadn't known that sexual fulfilment hadn't been her motive for following me from Oxford.

Her real motives became apparent in the small hours of the morning. There was an hour or so when both of us were pretending to be asleep, doing the deep, even breathing bit, but I was the better actor. When Caroline quietly eased herself out of bed her options were still open. If she had disturbed me a reference to her weak bladder would have been all that was necessary to put her in the clear. However, once she began a systematic search of the living-room her boats were burned. I allowed her to get well started before I joined her.

'Well, well, well,' I said pushing open the door. 'This is a surprise.'

It certainly came as one to Caroline. With the contents of an open drawer strewn about in front of her there was little point in her protesting her innocence. All the same, she was sufficiently quick-witted to seize on the lesser of two evils. She'd rather admit to being a thief than say what she was really doing.

'What the hell did you expect?' Her retort came out as a sneer, and she was quite prepared to use her naked body as a

47

weapon. 'You don't have the kind of sex appeal that bridges the generation gap.'

'I never thought that I had,' I answered mildly. 'I'd assumed it was a union of convenience. You wanted somewhere to sleep, and I wanted you.'

'Come off it, for Christ's sake,' Caroline scoffed. 'If a bed was all I was after, why should I latch on to you? I wouldn't have gone short of offers.'

'So you were only after my money?'

I'd decided to encourage her by appearing to be both shamefaced and resentful. This was the way I should have looked after her attack on twentieth-century man's most precious possession, his ego.

'What do you think? Let's face it, you don't have a great deal else to offer.' She paused a moment to allow the insult to register. 'What do you intend to do now?' she went on. 'Call for the police?'

Once again Caroline had played her cards very astutely. She'd neatly created a scenario which explained her present predicament and passed the problem on to me. Certainly, if I'd been as gullible as she must think I was, there was no way I'd have called in the law. It must have been quite gratifying for her to see my shake of the head, but she wouldn't have been nearly so keen on the smile which accompanied it.

'It was a good try,' I told her, 'but there's something you seem to have overlooked. Why don't you try to explain why you followed me from Oxford?'

This should have been my big moment, the instant when Caroline's world crumbled about her. It might even have happened if Caroline hadn't found the concealed compartment in the drawer where I kept my Colt Python.

OK, so I'd read plenty of books where a woman with a gun was little more than a joke. These were the ones where the heroes laughed nonchalantly before plucking the weapon from nerveless fingers, confident and secure in their male superiority. Perhaps I wasn't the stuff of which heroes were supposed to be made. When Caroline brought the Python up from her side where she'd been concealing it, I didn't feel at all like laughing, least of all nonchalantly. Nor did I even consider stepping forward to take the revolver from her. Her awkward grip on the gun might indicate a lack of expertise, but she'd managed to thumb off the safety-catch, and I knew precisely what would happen if she squeezed the trigger. Given time to think, I could even come up with the correct mathematical formulae. According to my rough calculations, and making due allowance for her inexperience, if Caroline shot at the centre of my chest from a range of ten feet, I was going to end up with a bloody mess where my head used to be. This struck me as a most persuasive argument for standing stock-still and listening attentively to whatever she might say. There was a brittle excitement about her which would have scared the pants off me if I'd been wearing any.

'Now, you bastard,' Caroline said, the excitement creeping into her voice as well. 'Back into the bedroom.'

I went back into the bedroom, stalked by Caroline, who was still keeping ten feet of clear space between us. The last six of them would all have been suicidal.

'Lie down on the bed,' she ordered. 'No, not like that. On your stomach.'

I rolled over with extreme reluctance, and this wasn't simply because I'd been taught never to turn my back on a lady. There were a lot of intertwined psychological patterns involved in killing somebody. If Caroline should decide to dispose of me, she'd find it much easier not to have me staring her in the eye.

'I hope you're comfortable,' she said, disappointing me by sitting on a chair at the foot of the bed, 'because you're staying there until you've answered some questions.'

'A woman of many parts,' I commented. 'Whore, sneak-thief and inquisitor. What other talents do you have?'

This wasn't empty bravado. Professionals were motivated by logic, necessity or expedience, but Caroline was likely to operate by whim. I'd no desire to become a victim, and I wasn't going to behave like one. This would merely give Caroline ideas. She showed her appreciation by cracking me on the ankle with the gun.

'I'm not interested in your opinions of me,' she told me. 'We're going to talk about you.'

'That's a very boring subject, I'm afraid.'

'Let me be the judge of that. You can start by explaining exactly who you are.'

'You know already. I told you in the King's Arms.'

This was when Caroline cracked me on the other ankle, proof that she intended to treat me like a victim whatever I did. Her sadistic tendencies obviously weren't confined to sex.

'That isn't what I meant, and you know it. What's your interest in Mandy Collison?'

'Incidental.' I had a set of bruised ankles to persuade me that a degree of co-operation was in my own best interests. 'The person I'm looking for is Vanessa Denny. Mandy was a close friend of hers, and they disappeared at the same time, so it seemed logical to pay a visit to the Robertses.'

It wasn't much of a trap but Caroline walked straight into it. Either that or she chose to ignore it. Vanessa's was a name she obviously recognized.

'You're working for Mr Denny?'

'That's right.'

'And what have you learned about sweet Vanessa?'

There was malice in her voice which could only have been developed by personal contact.

'Not a lot,' I admitted. 'She appears to have vanished into thin air.'

There was more I could have said, but I chose not to. Since Caroline had found the gun the whole situation had escalated, committing the two of us to a slippery, downward path which had very few side-turnings. Originally Caroline had come into my bed because she'd wanted to find out about me, who I was and what I did. This had entailed little more than

50

sex and snooping. Exposure plus the gun equalled interrogation, and we were coming dangerously close to the point where we went one step further. Whether she was aware of this or not, Caroline was making it virtually inevitable.

'What did the Robertses have to say?' she asked. 'Weren't they any help?'

'They'd never even heard of Vanessa. According to them, Mandy kept her friends to herself.'

There were a few seconds of silence while Caroline considered where to go next. This afforded me the opportunity to do the same. I was wondering whether a spot of aggression might be sufficient to kick me out of trouble.

'So what did they have to say?'

'If you're so interested why don't you go and ask them yourself? I'm tired of answering questions.'

My immediate reward was to feel the cold metal of the Python caressing the sole of my right foot.

'I don't know a great deal about guns, of course, so I can't really be sure,' Caroline said reflectively, 'but I should imagine that if I pulled the trigger now you'd probably lose most of your foot.'

And my lower leg as well. So much for aggression.

'They told me that Mandy was dead.' Although I wasn't exactly gabbling, I wasn't wasting any time in changing my mind. 'She was killed in a car crash in Norfolk.'

'And?'

The gun hadn't moved.

'They said there was another girl in the car with Mandy. So far she hasn't been identified.'

'In that case I'd better help you out.' The gun had gone now, but I still wasn't feeling particularly secure. 'As you may have guessed, the other corpse belonged to Vanessa. She and Mandy died in the car together.'

'Thanks for telling me.'

My gratitude was severely qualified because I didn't like the turn the conversation had taken. I was squinting back at Caroline over my left shoulder, and I could tell the precise

51

moment she decided to shoot me. For a few seconds she gnawed at her bottom lip while she tried to make up her mind, her forehead puckered in a frown. Then she came to the only possible conclusion, and the frown disappeared. There was only one thing she could do, which made two of us who realized it.

Although I started to roll as she levelled the Python, I was barely fast enough. My cheek actually felt the breeze the bullet made on its way into the pillow.

'Shit,' Caroline said elegantly. 'Why the hell couldn't you lie still?'

She had no intention of missing a second time. The frown had reappeared, her lower lip was between her teeth again and the gun was swinging round to zero in on me where I was lying on my back beside the bed. It didn't even occur to her that she might be in any danger, but naïveté wasn't sufficient to keep her alive. Although my spare gun was free of the clips beneath the bed, there was absolutely no margin for error. Caroline had a bloody great gun of her own, and this was a consideration which superseded any misguided thoughts of chivalry. I aimed where I knew I couldn't miss, and I kept on squeezing the trigger until I was positive there was no chance of Caroline sending any bullets back in my direction. The shame of it was, I'd had plenty of questions of my own that I'd wanted to ask.

'I thought it was female spiders who killed their mates after copulation.'

Gregson spoke with some relish, the same relish with which he'd examined Caroline's naked corpse. It was just my luck that he should be in charge of the disposal unit.

'Can it, will you,' I said. 'I'm not in the mood for your little witticisms.'

'Just think what the lads in blue would have made of this.' Gregson had ignored my plea, as I'd known he would. His self-appointed mission in life was to help bad taste to plumb new depths. 'You know what they'd have thought.'

'That's why I sent for you. I was hoping for a little tact and discretion.'

Gregson favoured me with the easy, amiable smile which was one of his most infuriating characteristics. It was virtually impossible to insult him, and he was completely immune to sarcasm.

'You'd better give me a few of the details, Philis old mate,' he told me. 'Pawson is probably on the way by now, and he'll expect to find everything shipshape and Bristol fashion.'

He accompanied his last remark with a leer at Caroline's blood-stained torso. I found him almost as funny as tertiary syphilis.

'Do you have a name to go with the corpse?' he asked.

I shrugged my shoulders.

'You can take your pick. All the documentation in her purse is in the name of Caroline Morris. At the car hire firm, though, she was Caroline Moore. At a rough guess, both names are equally phoney.'

Gregson nodded and scrawled something down on the form. Even unwanted bodies had to have their paperwork processed in triplicate.

'I suppose it's no good asking you for any other personal details.'

'None at all.'

'How about distinguishing marks?'

He was wearing his leer again.

'Why not go and take a look for yourself. She's hardly in any condition to object.'

'I will, Philis, I will,' Gregson promised. 'Let's see. The cause of death is fairly obvious, but so far I haven't heard anything about your reasons. Wouldn't she come across for seconds, or was there more to it than that?'

Although Gregson would have been quite content to continue questioning me in the same light-hearted vein he was interrupted by Pawson's arrival on the scene. For a minute or two he stalked around my flat without saying anything, poking his nose into everything and doing his best to make everybody nervous. Once he was satisfied that he'd established moral ascendancy he gave a jerk of his head to indicate I was to follow him out into the kitchen.

'Well, Philis?' he enquired once we were alone.

'You know almost as much as I do. The girl must have been keeping watch on the Robertses' house. She trailed me from Oxford and then picked me up. I caught her searching my flat.'

'And then you shot her. Was that strictly necessary?'

'Of course not.' The sarcasm came easily. 'I was bored and I didn't have anything else to do.'

'Perhaps I'd better rephrase the question, Philis.' Pawson was totally unmoved by my little outburst. 'I was wondering why you shot to kill.'

'Because at the time it seemed a much better idea than allowing her to kill me.' I was still annoyed. 'She'd already taken one potshot at me.'

'With your own gun?'

This was a definite reproof, and I deserved it.

'My own gun,' I agreed.

Pawson nodded and leafed through Gregson's report. It couldn't have told him very much.

'Have you drawn any conclusions from the incident?' he asked.

'You can scrub your Arab terrorist conspiracy theory. If there was any conspiracy, it was strictly amateur.'

'And?'

This wasn't nearly enough to satisfy Pawson.

'You can probably scrub Vanessa Denny as well. She's almost certainly dead.'

'Good.' Pawson had chosen the word advisedly. From where he stood, a dead Vanessa created far fewer problems than a kidnapped one. 'Keep me informed of any further developments. In return I'll arrange a rundown on this Morris girl.'

I watched him go in silence. There had been a moment

when I'd been tempted to mention that I was being employed by Denny, not the department, but I'd realized this wasn't worth the effort. Pawson wasn't simply aiming for the best of two worlds. He seemed to be achieving it as well.

CHAPTER VI

How do you set about telling somebody that his only daughter is dead? This was the question which preoccupied me for most of the journey to Harpenden the following morning, and I failed to come up with a satisfactory answer. I could think of no way to break the news gently. However circuitously I approached the subject, the harsh words would have to be spoken sooner or later. No amount of varnishing by me could alter the reality of what had happened. In the end I chose the coward's way out, presenting Denny with those few facts I'd gleaned and leaving him to draw his own conclusions. Although I omitted any mention of Caroline as not being strictly relevant, the implications of what Roberts had told me were as clear to Denny as they had been to me.

'I see,' he said quietly after a brief pause. 'So you think Vanessa is dead.'

'I'm afraid so,' I agreed. 'I'd be absolutely delighted if I was proved wrong but on the facts available it seems to be the only possible conclusion.'

Denny nodded. Many people might have mistaken his self-control for callousness, but I knew better. Although the news had hit him very hard, Denny wasn't the type to do his wailing and gnashing of teeth in public. This was something I admired him for.

'I wish I could disagree with you, Philis.' For a syllable or two Denny's control almost slipped, but he was quick to repair his defences. 'You say you've spoken to the local police?'

55

'Yes, I telephoned them first thing this morning. They were necessarily vague, but from what I can gather the age and build seem to match Vanessa's.'

'And?'

Denny had been exceedingly quick to spot my slight hesitation. I was being silly, because I knew it was something I'd have to tell him. It wouldn't be fair to allow him to walk in cold.

'Apparently the petrol tank exploded after the car went over the cliff,' I explained. 'Both bodies were severely burned. That was why the police were unable to issue a photograph or Identikit composite of the second victim.'

'But there is enough left for the body to be identified by a close relative? Somebody like a father, say.'

No matter how hard he tried, Denny's voice had become very tight.

'This was one of the things I discussed with the police. Rather than expose yourself to unnecessary distress, they suggest you might prefer to arrange for Vanessa's dentist to send them a copy of her dental chart. That would be sufficient for a preliminary identification.'

Somehow the words didn't come out quite right. Perhaps I lacked experience in displaying concern for other people's feelings.

'Mr Philis.' Denny's voice was suddenly firm and decisive. 'I appreciate what you and the police are endeavouring to do for me, but a dental match wouldn't be sufficient to satisfy me. If the second body is Vanessa's, I want to see it for myself, no matter what condition it may be in. I failed Vanessa as a father while she was alive, and I've no intention of doing the same in death.'

Although Denny had expressed himself poorly, I thought I understood what he meant. Hair-shirts and scourging might have gone out of fashion, but Denny had found himself the perfect substitute.

'That's your privilege, Mr Denny,' I told him. 'In fact, I did warn the police to expect you in person.'

56

'Good, but there's one other thing. I'd like you to accompany me.'

What the hell for? was my immediate reaction. However, it was a reaction I kept to myself. I knew he must have a good reason for his request.

'Fine,' I said. 'When would you like to start? I can drive if you like.'

Denny answered me with his first smile of the morning. It wasn't much of one but at least it was an improvement.

'That's very kind of you, Philis, but there's no need. Wealth does have its own small compensations.'

He was, as I discovered, referring to the helicopter which landed on the lawn half an hour later. With its assistance we were in Hunstanton in time for a late lunch.

I didn't see a great deal of Denny during the rest of the day. This wasn't simply because he was the principal and I was no more than a lowly menial. Any ordinary citizen in Denny's position would have been in and out of Hunstanton police station within a couple of hours. Denny, however, was a special case. He'd blown his trumpet in advance, and our brief journey by helicopter had been long enough for most of the top brass in the West Norfolk constabulary to decide on a day by the seaside.

This all seemed a bit rich for my blood. Besides, I didn't like mortuaries, so I elected to drift around on my own. Some of the time I spent in the company of the case officer. It was a spotty kind of conversation, as he kept on being summoned into the high level deliberations, but it was quite rewarding nevertheless. So was a little excursion to the site of the accident. Even without the confirmation provided by Caroline my suspicions would have been aroused. These, however, were something I'd no intention of sharing with Denny. Not unless he asked me outright.

The first real opportunity we had to talk together came in the early evening. The whisky on sale at the Le Strange Arms might not be up to the standard of Denny's private stock, but it was good enough, for all that. We were booked into the hotel for the night.

'I'm sorry you've been so neglected, Philis,' Denny was saying. 'All the same, I expect you heard the bad news.'

'I did. I'm very sorry it turned out this way.'

I was as well, even if I hadn't ever met Vanessa. Denny lived in too different a world for friendship to develop, but I'd already learned to respect him. Although he was hurting a lot, he'd come to terms with his loss, and he was determined to cope. The only real flaw in his façade was his guilt complex, and this was an attitude I probably understood better than most. I'd had occasion to feel the same in the past.

'I haven't seen where Vanessa died yet,' he told me. 'I'd like to.'

'Didn't the police take you?'

I was surprised. I'd assumed that this would be an integral part of the red-carpet treatment.

'They offered, but I didn't want to be surrounded by strangers when I went. I'd be grateful if you'd come with me, though.'

'Of course, but we'd better wait until the morning. You won't be able to see much in the dark.'

'It must have been dark when Vanessa died,' Denny pointed out. 'I'd prefer to go now.'

It wasn't simply dark on the beach. It was also bitterly cold, with a strong wind blowing in from the sea which must have originated somewhere in the Arctic. Fortunately we only had to trudge about a quarter of a mile through the fine sand from the hotel to the site of the accident. Even with the torches we'd borrowed at the hotel there wasn't a great deal to see on the beach itself. The police had tidied up most of the wreckage, and the sea had done the rest.

'Is there any way to reach the top of the cliff?' Denny enquired.

'Sure. There's some kind of a path where the beach huts end.'

The car park at the top was surfaced with short, springy

turf, and there was no mistaking where the car had gone over the edge. Although there were no skid marks it was impossible to miss the yawning gap in the guard rail. Once through that and the car would only have had another five yards to travel before the sheer thirty-foot drop.

Denny poked around for a few minutes, muttering and snorting to himself. Whatever his thoughts might have been he wasn't sharing them with me for the time being.

'Let's go back and have another drink,' he said abruptly, turning away from the cliff edge. 'I've seen all I want to see.'

Yet again, I'd no intention of arguing with him. The windswept cliff-top amply confirmed all my earlier reservations about holidays in February.

By nine o'clock we were back on the cliff again. Although it wasn't a great deal warmer than it had been the previous night, at least it was light. Denny himself appeared to have entered a new phase. The night before he'd been emoting. He hadn't said as much, of course, but I guessed that he'd been trying to relive in his own mind the last few minutes of his daughter's life. He'd been attempting to visualize what Vanessa must have been thinking as the car had smashed through the guard rail. Now, however, his brain was back in charge, and there was a new purpose to his prodding around. I stood back and left him to it. Even in my sheepskin coat I wasn't exactly sweating, and I was relieved when Denny eventually left the cliff edge and came over to where I was standing.

'They must have been travelling at a hell of a speed to crash straight through the guard rail,' he commented. 'It looks pretty substantial to me.'

'Appearances may be deceptive. If you take a closer look at some of the other concrete posts you'll notice that a lot of them are badly cracked. If the supports were weakened where Vanessa's car went through, they needn't necessarily have been travelling very fast.'

'That's precisely what the police told me.' Denny didn't

59

sound as though he placed a great deal of faith in the official version. 'As they didn't carry out any tests, I suppose we'll just have to accept their estimate. All the same, I'd be much happier if there were some skid marks to show the car had made some attempt to pull up.'

It wasn't hard to guess what Denny was leading up to.

'If you have any thoughts about suicide,' I said, 'you can forget them. It's a big car park, and it was dark. The girls probably didn't realize how close they were to the cliff until they actually hit the guard rail. By then it would have been too late to do anything.'

'Maybe,' Denny conceded. He didn't sound as though he believed me any more than I believed myself. 'It still doesn't explain what they were doing in the car park in the first place. Or why they were driving a stolen car.'

'That's something we'll probably never know.'

For a long moment Denny looked me straight in the eye. Then he slowly shook his head.

'If you think that, my friend, you're very much mistaken. Before I'm finished I intend to know every last detail of what happened to Vanessa.'

In the face of such conviction and determination there was nothing I could say.

'Is that where Gates lives?' Denny asked, changing the subject.

He was pointing to the row of cottages which stood by the entrance to the car park. The buildings were about two hundred yards from where we stood, opposite the old lighthouse which somebody had converted into a house.

'That's right,' I told him, 'but I very much doubt whether you'll find him at home. He works in a garage in Hunstanton.'

'How about his wife? She must have been there when the accident happened.'

'I don't know, but we can find out easily enough.'

Anything was better than standing on the cliff-top while the blood in my veins coagulated into ice. We might be heading away from the Le Strange, but at least the walk should start my circulation going again.

Mrs Gates was at home, and as soon as she opened her mouth it became obvious that she was a local woman. Norfolk might not boast the most melodious of regional accents, but it was a hell of a sight better than some.

'I thought you might be coming over when I saw you standing by the cliff,' she said by way of greeting. 'I must say, though, you don't look very much like policemen to me.'

'We're not,' Denny explained. 'I'm the father of one of the girls who died in the accident.'

'Oh, I'm so sorry.' There was no doubting the woman's sincerity. 'It was shocking. I couldn't believe it when Dyson came rushing back and told me what happened. Do come in, won't you? I put the kettle on when I saw you walking this way.'

Once we were ensconced in front of the fire Mrs Gates turned off the flow of words and bustled off to make tea. As soon as she'd gone Denny went over to the front window, staring morosely across the car park to where the tragedy had occurred. I preferred to watch Mrs Gates at work through the open kitchen door. She was quite good-looking in a solid sort of way, with a set of hips which suggested she must come of sound breeding stock. Despite her size she moved well, with a natural grace which was totally lacking in selfconsciousness. Even when she caught me looking at her she merely flashed me a friendly smile and continued with her tea-making. Guile and artifice probably had no place in her world.

When Mrs Gates returned to the living-room there was another minute or two of bustle while she handed round cups of tea. There were also some rather tasty home-made biscuits to go with the drink. I nibbled at one and left it to Denny to make the running. It was his show, and to date I wasn't absolutely sure why I was there.

'Well now,' Mrs Gates said brightly, at last settling herself into a chair. 'What can I do for you?'

61

'I'd like you to tell us what happened the night of the accident,' Denny told her. 'I read the statement your husband gave to the police, but I'd far rather hear it from your own lips. Police prose is on the flat side.'

Mrs Gates gave an embarrassed little laugh. She didn't really enjoy being the centre of attention.

'I don't know that there's a lot I can say. It was Dyson who saw it all.'

'Surely you must have heard or seen something, Mrs Gates.'

Denny had a soothing, persuasive tone of voice which he evidently reserved for such occasions, and it certainly worked the trick with Mrs Gates. Once she started she found she had quite a lot to say. It had been about midnight when her husband had first heard the car driving around in the car park. He was the lighter sleeper of the two, and Mrs Gates herself hadn't woken up until he'd slipped out of bed to go across to the window. It hadn't been until she'd heard the noise the car was making that she'd been tempted to follow his example. The night had been bitter, and she wouldn't have left her warm bed unless she'd thought something unusual was taking place.

'I don't suppose you get many cars coming here in winter,' Denny put in.

'We see a few, but they're mostly courting couples.' Mrs Gates gave another of her embarrassed laughs. 'We don't get many who go racing round and round the car park at that time of night. The car was going really fast.'

'And it went too near the edge of the cliff?'

Denny knew perfectly well that this wasn't what had happened but he was a good prompter.

'Oh no.' Mrs Gates was clearly reliving the drama of the night by now. 'The car drove round and round for a few minutes, then it stopped facing the sea. I thought it must be a young couple after all, and went back to bed.'

'How far away from the cliff did the car stop?'

'It's difficult to say, but Dyson told the police he thought it

62

must have been about fifty yards. Although it was a bit foggy, he could see the headlights shining out over the sea until they were turned off. Dyson had just come back to bed himself when the engine started again.'

'How long was the car stationary, Mrs Gates?'

This time I was the one who asked the question. I hadn't had access to the statements given to the police.

'It must have been almost five minutes. Dyson reached the window again just as the car went over the cliff. Then there was an explosion. The police say it must have been the petrol tank.'

The physical details had made Denny withdraw into himself, so I took Mrs Gates through the rest of her story. There wasn't a great deal more to it. Mr Gates had thrown on a coat and rushed out to see whether there was anything he could do to help, while his wife had run next door to telephone the police. After this, officialdom had taken over.

I grabbed myself another couple of biscuits to see me back to the hotel, thanked Mrs Gates for her hospitality and assistance, and ushered the still silent Denny to the door. There were other people living in the cottages who must have seen something, if not as much as Gates, but I'd already heard more than enough. So, I suspected, had Denny. I could almost hear his brain clicking over as we walked back to the Le Strange.

'Vanessa was a teetotaller,' Denny said. 'She took after her mother. She wouldn't even have a glass of wine with her meals or at parties.'

'I didn't know that.'

Although I knew perfectly well what Denny was getting at, I left him to it. I preferred to prove I didn't have any of Vanessa's bad habits by sipping my drink at the hotel bar. If the affair was to be taken any further it had to be Denny's decision.

'According to the post-mortem,' Denny continued grimly, 'both girls had been drinking heavily. They had more than

63

enough alcohol in their systems to make them drunk. It doesn't sound like my Vanessa at all.'

'People change,' I pointed out, 'especially at Vanessa's age. You said yourself that she seemed to become a different person after her mother's death.'

Denny treated me to a long, piercing look. He didn't appear to have a great deal of admiration for my stock of platitudes.

'I see,' he said.

Then he reached into the inside pocket of his jacket to bring out his cheque book. He had a gold pen to go with it and I watched while he filled out a cheque. When he'd finished, he tore it out and pushed it along the bar towards me. The cheque was for £500 and payable to me.

'That makes us square, Philis, apart from your expenses,' he said. 'You found Vanessa and that's what I hired you to do.'

I didn't play coy about accepting his offering. Nor did I bother with a pretty little speech of acceptance. Once I was satisfied that the cheque had been filled in correctly, I folded it neatly and tucked it inside my wallet. By then Denny was already at work on a second cheque. When he handed it to me I could see it was a duplicate of the first.

'What's that for?' I enquired.

'An opinion, if that's what it takes to obtain one from you.'

Although Denny was clearly angry, I couldn't help smiling.

'I'm flattered you should value me so highly, but my opinions come free.'

I didn't add that there were some people who would willingly pay not to hear them.

'So why haven't I been hearing any?' Denny demanded, still angry. 'Over the past couple of days you haven't come up with a single comment unless I've wrung it out of you.'

'That's true,' I admitted, 'but I thought this might be a good point to leave it all. You know Vanessa is dead; you know she died in a tragic accident. Why keep the hurt alive by doing any more digging and probing?'

'Because I don't know the reason for her death.' Denny almost snapped the words out. 'I thought I'd already explained that. I don't know why Vanessa was in Norfolk with Mandy Collison. I don't know why she was in a stolen car, and I don't know why she was so drunk she drove straight over a goddamned cliff. I've no intention of stopping until I do know. All I'm asking from you is an opinion about why it all happened. It doesn't seem to be too much to ask.'

I nodded my head in agreement. There was nothing else I could do.

'OK,' I said. 'I don't know the why any more than you do but if it's my opinion you want, you're welcome to it. I'd say your daughter was murdered. Somebody filled her and Mandy full of booze, brought them to the car park and then arranged for the car to take them over the cliff.'

If I'd expected Denny to be surprised, I would have been disappointed. He seemed almost gratified.

'Thank you, Philis,' he said. 'I'd come to exactly the same conclusion myself.'

Denny and I did the rest of our talking over a bottle upstairs in his room. Now we were talking murder there was no place for secrets, and I gave him an abbreviated version of my encounter with Caroline.

'So what do we do next?' Denny enquired once I'd finished. 'Go back to the police?'

'I don't think so, not yet at any rate. As far as they're concerned it was an open and shut case. We don't really have anything which is likely to make them change their minds.'

'Not even if we explain about you being followed back from Oxford?'

'Not even then,' I told him. 'Besides, that's not really a subject I care to discuss with the police. It would make life awkward for me and the department. Her car has been returned to the hire firm by now and her body will be very difficult to find.'

One of the things I liked most about Denny was that he didn't believe in beating about the bush. Instead of arguing, he dug into his pocket and fished out the second cheque again. It looked very attractive, waving under my nose.

'Originally you told me you were at my disposal for a fortnight. I want to rehire you for the next ten days on the same terms as before. Or, if you like, I'll better them. Go out and dig up some proof that the police can use.'

It took considerable effort to shake my head, and this wasn't simply because of the money I was turning down. Despite myself, I'd become involved. I didn't like unanswered questions any more than Denny did.

'I'm afraid it's not on, Mr Denny.'

'Why ever not? If it's more money you want, you can name your own price.'

'I only wish it was as simple as that. For a start, there's Mr Pawson to consider. He steered me in your direction because he thought there was a possibility that Vanessa's disappearance might eventually become departmental business. Now that no longer holds good. Pawson will want me out of it. He doesn't encourage his operatives to strike out on their own, especially when they might be meddling in police affairs.'

This must have been an objection which Denny had anticipated. He had his answer off pat.

'Just leave Mr Pawson to me.' He was speaking with the total confidence of wealth and power. 'He'll OK it if I speak to him nicely. One way or another he owes me quite a few favours. Is there anything else?'

'Only the fact that you'd be wasting your money. I'm not the right man for the job.'

'It's up to me how I choose to spend my money. Besides, you said more or less the same thing when we first met. It didn't stop you discovering what had happened to Vanessa.'

'That was luck.' I was being honest, not modest. 'What you want now is completely different. You're talking about a full-scale investigation, and that needs manpower. You might not be able to go to the police yet, but this is the kind of work Abercrombie's specialize in. I'd go back to them. I'm not likely to uncover much on my own, however much of my time you pay for.'

For a moment or two Denny didn't reply. He was too busy pouring us both a fresh drink.

'Let's get this straight, Philis,' he said when he was finished. 'It's your luck I want to hire. I've seen quite a lot of you over the past day or two, and what I've seen I like. You give me confidence.'

'That's very flattering. Unfortunately, it doesn't alter the fact that your confidence will be misplaced. I'm just not equipped to handle this kind of work.'

'Maybe.' Denny wasn't finished yet. 'All the same, if I manage to sort out Pawson and the manpower problem, you won't have any deep-rooted objections to working for me?'

It didn't take me very long to decide to shake my head. Curiosity was a human failing, and I was definitely human. I'd hate to walk away and never know why Vanessa Denny had been killed. Besides, Caroline had made sure my interest was personal. I always felt this way when somebody tried to kill me.

'Fine. I'll get on to Abercrombie's straight away. They can provide the men to do the spade-work, but you'll be the person in overall charge. How does that suit you?'

It suited me well enough for me to finally accept his cheque. Abercrombie's wouldn't be quite so enthusiastic about the arrangement, of course, but I had no doubt about Denny's ability to persuade them to play ball. He was the kind of man who usually had his own way.

CHAPTER VII

I didn't number any gentlemen farmers among my friends or
acquaintances. After a few minutes spent watching Alistair
Brown in action I began to understand why. I only had to
listen to what he was saying to the tractor driver to realize
that, in Brown's mind at least, feudalism was still alive and
flourishing. Ostensibly it was a friendly enough conversation, but it wasn't necessary to dig very far below the surface
to discover what was wrong with it. There was condescension
implicit in every word Brown spoke, a constant awareness of
the unbridgeable social gulf which separated him from his
employee. The worst of it was that the tractor driver agreed
with him. He was prepared to accept and endorse Brown's
assessment of himself as a member of the natural elite. He
didn't mind doing the forelock-tugging, cap-doffing bit provided it kept the boss happy. Quite possibly I might have had
a similar attitude if I'd lived in a tied cottage. Although both
men were using Christian names, this was nothing more than
window-dressing, and the true nature of the relationship was
apparent in every word which was spoken. Lord and master
had been talking to one another in much the same fashion for
the past several hundred years.

As Brown turned away from the tractor driver and began
splashing through the mud towards my car I decided I was
quite probably being grossly unfair. Perhaps I was simply
allergic to men with public-school accents and Savile Row
wellies. When Brown reached me I discovered something
else I was allergic to. The casual way he sized me up and then
dismissed me from any significant role in the overall scheme
of things went right up my nose.

'Are you the Fison's rep?' he enquired.

I carefully filed the insult away for future reference and
handed him my business card, the one which said I was a

private investigator. It may have been wishful thinking, but it didn't strike me as though Brown enjoyed what he read. A note of caution had entered his voice when he spoke again.

'What on earth have I done to bring you down on my back?' Although Brown was trying to sound jocular, he was making sure his voice didn't carry as far as the tractor driver. 'Don't tell me I'm behind with my alimony payments.'

'I really wouldn't know. I wanted to talk to you about the car you had stolen a few weeks back.'

All of a sudden Brown's smile was carefree again. He even managed a laugh.

'The number of questions I've had to answer, you'd think I'd stolen it myself. What's your interest?'

'It's a matter of insurance,' I explained vaguely.

Even if I'd liked Brown, I'd still have lied. Insurance claims sounded far more innocuous than murder investigations, and there was no point in revealing my hand until I had a better idea of precisely what I was investigating.

'I thought that had all been settled.' Brown was clearly puzzled. 'When I put in my claim I was told it would be quite straightforward.'

'It's not your insurance that concerns me. I'm making enquiries about one of the victims. It's standard practice when large personal accident policies are involved.'

Fortunately Brown knew even less about insurance than I did. I'd also managed to haul myself a rung or two up the social ladder. Reps and private investigators weren't the kind of people Brown wanted to drink with, but, after a few moments' consideration, he decided that in view of my connection with an insurance company I might just pass muster. This was when he suggested we adjourn to his local, a suggestion I seconded with alacrity. I always had preferred bars to muddy fields.

The pub was a local purely in the sense that it was situated in a village. It was the rural equivalent of executive bars in the city, operating the only effective kind of discrimination there

69

was. No horny-handed son of the soil would want to pay fifty pence for his pint of bitter, especially when it tasted as though it had come directly from a gnat's bladder.

Several of the lunchtime drinkers welcomed Brown when we went in, but he wasn't proud enough of me to indulge in any introductions. He preferred to hide me away in a quiet corner while he went up to the bar to order our drinks. He didn't seem to be in any particular rush to rejoin me either.

While Brown went through the social round up at the bar I sat back and allowed my dislike to develop. It was growing in direct proportion to the length of time I spent being nearly in his company. Unfortunately, I still had no real peg to hang it on apart from the fact that his whole attitude rubbed me up the wrong way. I was sure there were an awful lot of people who wouldn't have reacted to Brown in the same way. Many unprejudiced observers would have agreed with Brown and classified him as a natural gentleman. Mothers with daughters to marry off would automatically give him a prominent place on their short lists of suitable candidates. Come to that, a lot of the daughters would probably do the same, because he was hardly physically repulsive. He was tall and blonde and clean-cut, and totally committed to growing old gracefully. Throw in a few hundred acres of prime farm land, and the Porsche he had in the car park, and you didn't have the kind of package which was likely to put women off.

Everything Brown had to say once he'd eventually joined me proclaimed him to be the total innocent. He'd been drinking at another of his favourite watering-places, the Rose and Crown in Snettisham, and when he'd left at closing time his Allegro had been missing. He'd gone back inside to telephone the police, and this had been the limit of his involvement. The next he'd heard was that the vehicle had been found at the bottom of Hunstanton cliffs with two bodies inside. His unspoken attitude was that this was the fate deserved by anybody who stole his property. He also seemed proud of his foresight in not driving his Porsche or Range Rover to the Rose and Crown on the night in question. There was nothing the least bit suspicious about his story, something I found rather disappointing.

'That seems straightforward enough,' I said. 'I gather both girls were complete strangers.'

'One of them was,' Brown corrected me. 'The last I heard the police still hadn't managed to identify the other body. The photograph I was shown wasn't anybody I knew. Mind you, I wouldn't have minded if she was as attractive as that in real life.'

Brown flashed me an all-boys-together type smile which I ignored. It wasn't all that different from Roberts's leer when he'd been telling me about his experiences with his sister-in-law.

'The police know who the other girl was now,' I told him. 'Her name was Vanessa Denny.'

While I was fishing in my wallet, Brown was busy shaking his head.

'The name doesn't ring any bells.'

'How about this?'

I handed him the photograph Denny had given me. Brown seized the opportunity to shake his head again.

'I'm afraid not,' he said. 'I'm sure I'd remember her if I'd seen her.'

'OK,' I said, retrieving the photograph. 'There's just one last question. Do you have any idea at all why the girls picked on your car? I gather the Rose and Crown was quite busy that night. There must have been plenty of other vehicles to choose from.'

Brown shrugged.

'Pot luck, I suppose. Besides, I was fool enough to leave my keys in the ignition. The police seem to think they were joy-riders, looking for any vehicle they could lay hands on. Mine happened to be the easiest.'

'That's what they told me.'

Neither of us had a great deal more to say to each other. I tried hard to think of more pertinent questions, while Brown made no secret of his desire to have done with me and find

71

more congenial company. Once he'd abandoned me in favour of his cronies at the bar I didn't linger for very long myself. I knew my place in life, and this definitely wasn't it. I hoped I'd have better luck at the Rose and Crown in Snettisham.

It was only half an hour before kicking-out time when I reached the Rose and Crown. Apart from a couple up at the bar, and half a dozen other customers grouped around the blazing fire, the main room was empty. The barmaid, a young girl with the face of an angel and a body which was a couple of stones overweight, was rinsing glasses and looking bored. After I'd ordered a drink I tried to bring a little excitement into her life by showing her the same card I'd given to Brown.

'You're a detective?'

The pronounced Norfolk accent was more in keeping with her body than her face.

'That's right,' I told her. 'I represent an insurance company. I'm making enquiries about a car which was stolen from your car park a few weeks back.'

'You mean Mr Brown's?'

'That's the one. I don't suppose you happened to be here the night it was stolen?'

'I'm afraid I wasn't. I only work lunchtimes.'

'Is there anybody around who was working that night?'

'I wasn't working, but I was here the night poor Alistair lost his car.'

It was a pleasant, deep-timbred voice, and there was a mocking note on the 'poor Alistair'. I turned slowly on my stool to face the woman who was seated at the far end of the bar with her companion. Although this was the first time I'd glanced in her direction, I'd been aware of her since the moment I'd stepped into the pub. And this wasn't simply because she was the only female customer.

'Perhaps you can help me, then.'

'I'm sure I can.' Her smile lent the words added signifi-

72

cance. 'It can't be now, though – I'm late for my appointment at the hairdresser's as it is. I'll be in here at eight this evening if you're interested.'

She was so sure of me that she'd swung off her stool and was heading for the door before I had a chance to reply. Her escort, a tall, bronzed young man who looked as though he was ninety-nine parts muscle to one part brain, tagged dutifully along behind. Before he went through the door, he spared time to shoot me a poisonous look. When I turned back to my drink, I discovered the barmaid was laughing at me.

'OK, OK,' I said defensively. 'I didn't realize I was being that obvious.'

'There's no need to apologize. Lady Laura has that effect on everybody in trousers.'

There was no malice in her voice, only admiration.

'Lady Laura?' I queried.

'It's a kind of nickname,' she explained. 'The title is false, but the money is real.'

I did my best to look as though she was telling me something new.

CHAPTER VIII

During the afternoon I made one or two further calls, covering ground the police had covered before me, and all I learned was that they'd been as thorough as I'd expected them to be. This was just as well because my heart wasn't really in what I was doing, and I found it rather disquieting to realize how much I was looking forward to the evening. Perhaps it really was true that absence made the heart grow fonder.

It was almost six years since Laura and I had first tumbled into bed together and nearly five since I'd last seen her. She'd been working for SR(2) as a courier when we'd met and this had been back in the good old days when it had still been possible to have normal relationships with female members of the department. While it had lasted ours had been much better than normal. Although it had started casually enough, prompted by little more than mutual physical attraction, we'd soon discovered that we took as much pleasure in each other's company out of bed as we did in it. Under other circumstances our relationship might have developed into something more permanent but romanticism and the department didn't mix. Laura never actually put it into words but she made it quite clear that she'd no intention of becoming seriously involved with somebody who was likely to return home minus an arm, leg or any other essential part.

We'd enjoyed what we had while we could and when we could and we'd kept it honest. Neither of us had needed to pretend to the other or make unnecessary demands. Because of this there had been no jealousy and when Laura had told me she was leaving the department to get married I hadn't tried to argue with her. I hadn't asked who her husband to be was or what he did. We'd been to bed together one last time as a kind of gesture to times shared and remembered, then we hadn't seen each other again. Later on, when I'd heard on the departmental grapevine that her husband had died of cancer, I'd been tempted to look Laura up but Pawson was keeping me busy at the time and I'd never got around to it. At the back of my mind had been the suspicion that people, like places, never had quite the same flavour when they were revisited. It seemed I might have been wrong.

In Norfolk they evidently did their serious drinking at night. The Rose and Crown was much busier than it had been at lunchtime, and when I arrived Laura was already holding court with three husky young men grouped around her. Rather than intrude I took my drink across to where the landlord was standing with a group of friends. He wasn't able to shed any new light on the theft of Brown's car, or on the girls who had stolen it, but at least our brief conversation helped me to pretend I was in the pub on business. This self-

74

deception wasn't quite so easy to maintain once I was at a table, sitting back in the shadow where my interest wouldn't be too apparent. Even from a distance Laura was worth watching. It was difficult to tell, and totally unimportant, but I guessed she might be closer to forty than thirty. She had her hedonism to keep her young.

It was only a couple of minutes before Laura disbanded her group of admirers with a few laughing words and started across to where I was sitting. The only one of the group who attempted to follow her was her companion of lunchtime, and she disposed of him with clinical cruelty.

'Don't be so tiresome, Tony,' she said in a clear, carrying voice. 'Do you have to follow me around like a pet poodle?'

'But, Laura . . . ' Tony began, flushing angrily.

'But nothing.' Laura's voice was as distinct as ever and she was attracting a wide audience. 'As you seem unable to take a hint, I'll spell it out for you. There's nothing here for you. Why don't you go back and play in your own league?'

Somebody at one of the other tables sniggered, and Tony's face turned a brick red. For a moment he looked as though he might say something in reply. Then he thought better of it and swung angrily away. Laura was too busy arranging herself in a chair to pay any attention to him as he stormed out of the pub.

'Did I embarrass you?' she asked, tossing back her mane of tawny brown hair and giving me a wicked smile.

'You know you did.' I was keeping my voice low. It wouldn't do a great deal for my cover for people to realize we already knew each other. 'Is this new bitchiness an essential feature of the widow Cunningham?'

'Definitely.' We were already settling back into the conversation patterns which old friends never seem to lose no matter how long they're apart. 'Besides, I've been very patient with Tony. If he didn't have a skin like a rhino, he would have got the message long ago. His trouble is that he fancies himself as the local stud. He can't understand why I don't leap at the opportunity to climb into bed with him.'

'You mean you haven't?'

'Of course not, darling.' Laura put one hand on top of mine. 'I've been saving myself for you.'

Despite the sarcastic tone, this was an invitation of sorts, an acknowledgement that the old attraction still worked both ways. All the same, it was a theme we had to shelve temporarily. As a couple of locals had moved over to sit at the table next to ours, it seemed advisable to drop back into my assumed role and ask the questions which were the supposed reason for my visit to the Rose and Crown. Unfortunately, Laura didn't have anything to add to what I'd already learned from the police, the landlord of the Rose and Crown and Brown himself. I doubted whether anyone who had been present that night was likely to provide any revelations.

Once I'd finished with the questions, I retreated into small talk and left it to Laura to make the next positive move. She was the one with a reputation to protect. Or lose, as the case might be. It was a quarter of an hour before she accepted her cue.

'I haven't eaten yet,' she announced. 'Have you?'

'Not yet,' I admitted.

For a moment she reminded me of another woman in another pub.

'I thought you had a hungry look about you. Finish your drink and I'll show you how domesticated I can be.'

I already knew and this was one of the reasons I wasn't slow to accept the invitation.

From the outside Laura's home looked like an ordinary cottage, built of the same local carstone as most of the older buildings in the village. Inside, it was a different story, and the exterior walls and roof were about all that remained of the original structure. Her little cottage in the country, or cottages, since two buildings had been knocked into one, had been converted into something which wouldn't have been out of place in the pages of *Homes and Gardens*. What was more, the conversion had been undertaken with taste, avoiding any overtones of cloying femininity. Whereas Denny's little spread at Harpenden was self-consciously opulent, Laura's was luxuriously comfortable. It would have made the ideal pied-à-terre for a bachelor of either sex.

While Laura busied herself in the kitchen I sipped a drink and examined the contents of her bookcase. This had always been something of an experience and in the past I'd often accused her of being a literary dustbin. Her stock defense had been that she had wide-ranging tastes and the present selection seemed to bear this out. On her shelves Barbara Cartland rubbed shoulders with Iris Murdoch, James Herriott with Jean Paul Sartre. The only evidence of any contribution from her late husband was a couple of weighty tomes on marketing techniques.

I didn't have as long to browse as I'd expected. It was only twenty minutes before Laura had rustled up a couple of ham omelettes which could have floated to the table on their own and followed them with her own version of crepes suzettes. When we'd finished we did the washing up together, the price Laura had always demanded of me in return for her doing the cooking.

It was only after we'd gone back into the living-room with our coffee that our conversation became at all meaningful. During the meal, by unspoken agreement, we'd kept our conversation inconsequential, circling around the two main areas which interested us. Now, however, they couldn't be ducked any longer. Because I managed to get my question in first it was Laura who started the explaining. Although she made no attempt to present it as a love-match, it seemed her marriage had been a happy one. Certainly there had been a great deal of mutual affection. Derek Cunningham had been almost thirty years older than his wife but from what Laura said this had been more of an asset than a drawback. While she didn't give many details, and I wouldn't have wanted to hear them, the partnership had worked well. And, as Laura quite candidly admitted, Derek's money hadn't done anything to harm it. She'd liked the life-style and she'd liked the new circle of friends she'd made, which was why she'd stayed on in Norfolk after Derek's death.

'So you haven't been tempted to come back to London?'

'Not really,' Laura answered. 'I do have the odd weekend shopping spree up in town every so often but I'm always glad to get back here. I'm a big fish in a little pool. It's good for my ego.'

'I gathered that you had a certain local notoriety. From what the barmaid at the Rose and Crown told me, you're the prime target for every red-blooded male in the district.'

'Now I think of it, I suppose Tony hasn't been the only man to show a degree of interest.'

Laura said this this with a laugh which disclaimed any attempt at false modesty. She attracted interest wherever she went and she knew it because Laura hadn't missed out on her fair share of female vanity. She was a woman whose whole was much better than the individual parts. If you ticked her features off one by one, Laura didn't have anything plenty of other women couldn't match or improve upon. Throw them all together in one five foot ten package and you had somebody who was noticed whatever the competition.

'How about you, Philis?' Laura asked. 'I couldn't believe it when you came walking in through the door of the pub, especially when you launched into that terrible private eye routine. What dark deeds bring you to this neck of the woods?'

She was rather surprised when I proceeded to tell her. Despite the security clearance she'd had prior to her marriage, she knew I wouldn't have said a word to her if I'd been on official business. As I wasn't, there was no harm in telling her the lot and she made a good listener.

'You'll be in the area for a few days, will you?' she said when I'd finished.

'It looks that way.'

'And will I be seeing any more of you?'

Neither of us had any real doubts about my reply. If I hadn't had to get back to the Le Strange in case there were

78

any messages waiting for me, I would have reassured her properly there and then.

Although it was only a six- or seven-mile drive to my hotel, the Le Strange, it had started to snow with great, heavy flakes which effectively reduced visibility to a few yards. The drunks who had been kicked out of their local hostelries didn't do a great deal to improve matters, and by the time I reached the hotel I was in a foul mood. Mostly it was frustration. I hadn't wanted to leave Laura and knowing that she'd wanted me to stay hadn't made departure any easier.

Finding a strange woman lying on my bed at the hotel temporarily shelved all thoughts of Laura. I wasn't particularly quiet going in, and I'd switched on the light before I'd realized she was there, but I didn't disturb her. It only took me a few seconds to realize she wasn't the kind of woman I wanted on my bed, even if she came as a gift. I was never turned on by women who snored with their mouths wide open, especially when they displayed a set of tobacco-stained dentures and smelled strongly of whisky. Whoever she was, she was well into middle age, and she'd gone to considerable pains to conceal whatever feminine charms she might have possessed. Unless I'd been missing out, heavy tweed suits, thick woollen stockings and brogues hadn't been featured in any of the major fashion shows.

Nor were any of the parts which were uncovered much of an improvement. The close-cropped grey hair looked as though it had either been gnawed by rats or hacked by the woman herself after a hard drinking bout. The skin of her face was wrinkled and seamed. Her hands were large and masculine, with nails which had been bitten down to the quick.

I didn't immediately disturb her slumbers. There was a portmanteau-sized handbag on the floor beside the bed and I decided to look inside it before I asked her what the hell she was doing in my room. The half-bottle of Johnny Walker wasn't much help, but her purse was far more informative.

After I'd examined her driving licence I sat down on the bed and gave one wool-covered knee a friendly squeeze. When the woman's eyes opened they looked rather like AA route maps, lots of red lines on a yellow background.

'Are you the Mrs Robinson they wrote the song about?' I asked.

'Very funny,' she said, knocking my hand off her knee. 'Where have you been all night?'

'Pursuing my enquiries,' I told her.

'And what have you come up with so far?'

'Not a lot,' I admitted.

Mrs Robinson snorted to show that this was no more than she'd expected. I'd read the reports she'd written for Denny, so I knew she must be good at her job, but this didn't necessarily mean I'd enjoy our association. However, this was something I'd have to discover at a later date. At breakfast the next morning there was a message from Pawson waiting for me. It said he wanted to see me as soon as I could get back to London.

CHAPTER IX

The police advised motorists not to set out; the radio bulletins talked about the worst weather since 1963, and gave impressive lists of major roads which were completely impassable. All over the country people were being frozen, flooded or frostbitten, but it never occurred to me to delay my journey. I knew Pawson would never accept a little inclement weather as an excuse for failing to answer his summons. If necessary, he'd expect me to put on snowshoes and cover the hundred-odd miles to London on foot.

The long hazardous drive gave me plenty of time to work at my resentment. Admittedly, I could hardly blame Pawson for the treacherous road conditions, the ghastly Mrs Robinson, or my frustrations of the previous night, but his brusque summons did give me some excuse for my anger. As Pawson had given me no indication why he wanted me in London, I had to work at three of four different scenarios which would cover most eventualities. All of them would have afforded me plenty of scope for some righteous indignation and biting sarcasm. The point I hadn't allowed for in my calculations was that Pawson might have anticipated my reaction to his message. When I eventually arrived in his outer office I discovered he wasn't even in the building.

'Where the hell is he, then?' I demanded.

'He has a meeting at the American Embassy,' his secretary explained.

'That's marvellous, isn't it? He drags me back to London at five minutes' notice, I risk my life driving here, and Pawson doesn't even have the common courtesy to be waiting for me when I arrive.'

The secretary was leaning her head on her hand and wearing the expression of somebody who had heard it all before. Quite possibly she had.

'Mr Pawson told me to tell you he'd be back in an hour, Philis. To save time, he wanted you briefed before the two of you met. You'll find all the relevant information on your desk.'

I left, muttering darkly under my breath, and stamped down the stairs to my office. However, as Pawson must have anticipated, my anger began to dissipate once I saw what was waiting for me. To begin with, the evaluation hadn't originated within SR(2) itself. Although it was inside one of the departmental folders the heading of each sheet had been carefully snipped off and all cross-references had been laboriously blocked out. I'd seen enough similar reports in the past to recognize what I was looking at. We quite frequently acquired information from other agencies, both friendly and hostile, which hadn't passed through official channels. Both the layout and phraseology of the document in front of me bore the unmistakable stamp of the FBI. This in itself seemed sufficient reason to put my bad temper into cold storage until

81

I actually confronted Pawson.

What was more, the report made interesting, if unusual, reading. The frontispiece was a blown-up photograph in colour. It showed a line of young people of both sexes standing in a derelict street in an unidentified American city. All of them wore symbolic sackcloth and ashes, and carried placards which were expressly designed to bring good cheer to any onlookers. I didn't bother to read all of them, but the one at the front, held by a young black whose facial expression matched his message, seemed fairly representative. 'THE WICKED SHALL BE TURNED INTO HELL,' it began cheerfully. 'AND ALL THE NATIONS THAT FORGET GOD FOR IF THEY WILL NOT OBEY, I WILL UTTERLY PLUCK UP AND DESTROY THIS NATION SAITH THE LORD. AND SHALL NOT MY SOUL BE AVENGED ON SUCH A NATION AS THIS? WHOSO DESPISETH THE WORD SHALL BE DESTROYED.' Although I wasn't too happy about some of the punctuation, there was no missing what the youth was trying to say, especially as some of the most important words, like HELL, DESTROY and AVENGE, had been picked out in red. There was no comment at all beneath the photograph, and none was necessary.

The section which followed was general in nature, and dealt with the so-called Jesus Revolution in the United States in the late '60s and early '70s. This had been the time when hundreds of thousands of young Americans had suddenly become turned on by religion, and had gone around raising one finger heavenwards instead of the traditional two.

For the most part the movement had been outside, and quite separate from, the traditional churches. Hundreds of new communes and sects had sprung up the length and breadth of America, each of them with their own particular interpretation of what Jesus had really meant. It was a time when strip-clubs had been converted into chapels, drug addicts had become high on God, and all manner of excesses had been committed in the name of religion. It was a subject I'd never studied before, and I found much of it quite amusing. My special favourites were the Christian Surfers, who received a brief mention in the report. As far as I found gather, their faith had been firmly based on the revelation that the perfect wave didn't necessarily equal total fulfilment.

However, there was nothing at all amusing about the sect which was the subject of the main body of the report. One of the most useful things about the Bible was that it said so many different things in different places that it could be used to provide support for almost anything as long as the texts were picked carefully enough. The founder of the Messengers of God, a one-time fundamentalist preacher called Sidney Elkhart, had done precisely this when he'd established the new sect in 1966. He'd elected to ignore everything Jesus had said about love and concentrate on the stronger stuff. Consequently, the God he'd presented was the god of the sword, who brought wrath and destruction to all who opposed his will. By this, of course, Elkhart had meant anybody who didn't agree with his own particular interpretation of the Bible.

Even so, the Messengers made relatively little impact during the first few months of their existence. Having gathered a nucleus of fifty or so converts around him, Elkhart had appeared to run out of missionary zeal. A wealthy businessman had donated a few acres of scrubland in southern California, and a commune was established, where Elkhart settled down to enjoy the pleasures of the polygamy he also preached.

However, other members of the sect weren't quite so complacent and contented. Notable among them was Elkhart's own brother, David. He could see the opportunities which were open to the Messengers if they were properly organized. Disruption of the services in other local Californian churches might be fun, but David favoured a far more aggressive approach. Whereas his elder brother had envisaged little more than a simple, self-sufficient community, David was all in favour of expansion. He knew that new converts meant new sources of cash.

As the report went on to say, it was unlikely that anybody would ever learn the precise details of how the argument was eventually resolved. All the same, it wasn't difficult to read between the lines. It was a matter of record that Sidney Elkhart was shot dead during a trip to San Diego. A few weeks later, three more of David's most vociferous opponents simply vanished without a trace. These occurrences were suspicious enough to attract the attention of the local sheriff's office but, despite a lengthy investigation, nothing could ever be proved. After the investigation had closed and the dust had settled only one indisputable fact emerged. David Elkhart had taken his brother's place as the spiritual leader of the tiny church of the Messengers of God.

David had had no intention of allowing it to remain tiny for long. The original commune was disbanded, and the missionaries were dispatched to major cities across the States. By now the Jesus Revolution was gathering steam and the pickings were easy, provided the young were told what they wanted to hear. Many of the Jesus freaks were the old flower-people and hippies, and what the Messengers had to say must have sounded like music to their ears. David Elkhart hadn't simply offered religion. He'd offered them an alternative way of life, a new life style which was isolated, and insulated, from the rest of the community and in which Mammon, institutions and hard work had no place. He preached against sinful America and forecast its imminent doom. He railed against politics and politicians, business and businessmen, finance and financiers. He'd offered the young an opportunity to continue believing what they believed already while providing them with biblical justifications for their beliefs. They could drop out and feel holier-than-thou at the same time.

Given these advantages it was hardly surprising that the ranks of the Messengers had soon shown a dramatic increase. Cynics might point out that Elkhart lived remarkably well for somebody who was supposed to despise worldly wealth. Certainly, he hadn't been too proud to accept any hand-outs which were going from the very people he said he despised. He had also shown a marked preference for well-to-do converts who, naturally, put all their belongings into the communal pool. None of this had seemed to matter to the faithful, or to the converts who had continued to flow in.

Unfortunately, success had brought attendant problems. It hadn't been long before active opposition to the sect had begun to grow, particularly in its birthplace, California. Unlike Billy Graham and the other evangelists, simple affirmations of faith hadn't been sufficient for Elkhart. When he or one of his missionaries converted somebody they intended him to stay converted.

Furthermore, Elkhart had soon recognized a truth which was to be exploited at Synanon and by Sun Myung Moon. To begin with, of course, he had relied on attacks on the established order and his own personal charisma to increase membership. It took him time to realize that this was only the ground-bait. The real strength of the Messengers lay in the sect's organization, in the communes, or 'family-centres' as Elkhart preferred to style them. Once there converts were completely isolated from any competing forces. They became totally dependent both on the community and on the approval of their peers.

Consequently, Elkhart changed his strategy slightly. His all-pervading influence remained, in writing, on film and by personal visits, but, this apart, the centralized structure was deliberately played down and kept in the background. Emphasis was placed on personal contact and the illusion was created that each commune was a distinct entity, loosely bound into the overall structure of the Messengers only by Elkhart himself. There were leaders, people within each commune who reported directly to Elkhart and were responsible for enforcing his wishes, but they had no titles and no official standing. Another illusion was created. Problems were solved communally, with everyone entitled to their say. It was sheer coincidence that some voices carried more weight than others.

When it came to recruitment, prospective converts were invited to spend a weekend at one of the family-centres, to sample the pleasures of communal living. Special programmes were arranged to make sure they enjoyed themselves. However, it was stressed that part-time membership was impossible, a tactic which effectively scared off the faint-hearted but exercised a powerful attraction for many young people to whom commitment was a brand new experience. It was all or nothing and within the communes group-pressures could be relied upon to act as a stabilizing influence. In this respect, Elkhart realized that the self-criticism sessions were vitally important, dragging any potential misgivings out into the open before they could become a threat. Only when they were considered committed were followers allowed to leave the womb of the commune to start, proselytizing themselves.

As most of the sect's recruits were youngsters in their late teens and early twenties, the majority of protests had come from parents. In part this had been a natural reaction to seeing children removed from their homes to live in one of the Messengers' communes where they were taught to attack all the values their parents held dear. Mainly, however, it had been outrage at the methods employed by the sect. In California anxious mothers and fathers formed an anti-Messengers action group which soon had branches across the country. Court cases were brought against the Messengers charging them with drug abuse, hypnotism and forcible abduction. In retaliation, Elkhart had initiated counter-suits charging libel and slander.

In themselves these attacks had posed little real threat to Elkhart because supposition and proof were two different things. There were, of course, failures, people who became disenchanted with the sect. Even so, they'd seemed strangely reluctant to discuss the more dubious aspects of the Messengers' activities. Their parents had maintained that they were too frightened to talk. According to the report, their fears had almost certainly been justified.

Only two ex-Messengers had expressed any willingness to co-operate with the authorities. One of them, a young man called Paul Conrad, had been sufficiently disillusioned to be quite outspoken in his attacks on his former brethren. His accusations received a fair amount of newspaper coverage, but he'd made his biggest headlines for quite another reason. One morning he'd put his hand into his parents' mailbox to collect the letters, and when he'd pulled it out a four-foot-long diamondback rattlesnake had come with it. He'd died on the way to hospital. The only other potential witness against the Messengers had abruptly changed her mind after her three-month-old baby had been kidnapped. The FBI were sure the child had been removed to one of the communes where it was being held hostage against the mother's good behaviour.

Elkhart's major problem had been his own greed. His preference for rich converts was all very well, but wealthy children had meant wealthy parents. They'd had sufficient influence and political clout to keep the pot boiling. Besides, the authorities had become interested on their own account, and they'd tried a different approach. Whereas the parents were emotive, the Attorney-General's offices in the states of New York and California had been far more practical. The parents had proved that a direct frontal attack would have little effect. The authorities had favoured a sneak attack, hitting Elkhart where it would hurt most, and they'd handed the investigation over to the Charity Frauds Bureau.

Although this had been a masterstroke of a kind, it had come too late. Elkhart had had no intention of standing still to be hit. The Messengers had introduced him to the good life, succeeding far beyond his wildest dreams. He'd absolutely no intention of seeing it all go to waste.

The excuse he'd used was the comet Kohoutek. For Elkhart this had been no lump of rock shooting around in space. It had been a message to the Messengers from God. According to what he preached the comet signalled the beginning of the end for the United States. Unlike other sects such as the Jehovah's Witnesses, Elkhart hadn't been fool enough to set any deadline for Doomsday. He maintained that God was simply warning the faithful. He was telling them that the ultimate catastrophe was on its way and that it was time for them to move on. America might be irretrievably doomed, but other countries were not quite so far along the road to ruin. If they listened to what the Messengers had to say they might possibly be saved. The faithful had listened and they'd obeyed. More than ten thousand hard-core members had departed from the States, scattering to the four corners of the Earth to continue their work as missionaries. Elkhart, of course, had been among them. Never one for understatement, he'd referred to the emigation as 'the second Exodus'.

This took me to the end of the second section of the report, and I had Anne bring me in coffee and a sandwich before I started on the final part. I didn't find it nearly as interesting as what had gone before, mainly because it was far more technical. I was no psychologist, and most of the fancy jargon used in the evaluation of David Elkhart passed way above my head. Nevertheless, the general principles were easy enough to understand. I'd spent enough time around Pawson to know exactly what megalomania meant.

CHAPTER X

'I assume you've been through the report, Philis.'

'I have.'

Pawson nodded. He was sitting half-turned away from me, fiddling with a pencil while he looked out of the window. It had stopped snowing, but a strong wind was blowing snow from the roof-tops in little flurries. Down in Norfolk it would be drifting.

'It makes for quite interesting reading, doesn't it?'

'Fascinating,' I agreed, 'but I'm not quite sure how it

applies to me. The last I heard I was supposed to be working for Denny.'

'You are, Philis, you are. I'm merely pointing you in the right direction.'

Pawson was in one of his relaxed and jovial moods. As always, he'd worked at my curiosity, throwing me a few scraps of information which were just sufficient to whet my appetite for more. One day, I suspected, this curiosity was likely to get me killed.

'So where do the Messengers of God fit in with Vanessa Denny?' I asked.

'To be honest, I'm not quite sure at the moment. All I do know is that your ex-girlfriend, the one you shot, used to be one of the Messengers. The FBI had her fingerprints on file. Her real name was Caroline Winters.'

'I thought she was English. She certainly didn't have an American accent.'

'She wouldn't have. Her father was part of the brain drain. He went to Santa Barbara about eight years ago to work for an electronics firm. Something to do with silicon chips.'

I lit myself a cigarette and tried the new pieces of the jigsaw to see how they fitted. It didn't take me very long to realize they matched pretty well. Pawson allowed me a few seconds before he gave me a jog.

'Well?' he prompted. 'Does the information help?'

'It helps a lot,' I told him, 'but there's one point I'd like you to clear up. I'm still not sure who I'm working for. What's the department's interest in all this?'

'Peripheral and strictly unofficial. As far as I'm concerned, you're on holiday, and I've authorized your private arrangement with Denny.'

'But?'

Pawson tilted back his chair and turned to look out of the window again, watching the patterns made by the whirling snow. Somehow it didn't look as white as it had done in Norfolk.

'Ours is a special responsibilities section,' he said slowly.

'It probably sounds pretentious, but we do have a duty to the government and to the public who elected it. I don't like what I've heard about the Messengers of God. They're a nuisance we can well do without.'

I nodded.

'If half of what I've read is true, I couldn't agree more.'

'That's only part of it, Philis. The problem as I see it is that they don't fall within our jurisdiction. There's no possible way I can justify taking official action against them. On the other hand, I can justify your temporary association with Denny. In fact, I've already done so. If his daughter was murdered and the Messengers of God were involved, it's only reasonable for me to give you all the unofficial support I can. Denny's providing the finance and manpower. I'm prepared to offer you any technical assistance you may need. You'll also have my full backing for whatever you decide to do, provided, of course, it's not totally irresponsible. I know how you work best, and I can't see any sense in cramping your style.'

Although it had been said in a roundabout way, this didn't affect my appreciation of what Pawson was offering me. I'd have far more freedom of action if I knew he'd vouch for me to the police. I only had the one reservation.

'Isn't the connection rather tenuous?' I asked. 'It's fairly safe to assume that Caroline Winters was involved in the deaths of the two girls, but this doesn't necessarily implicate the Messengers of God. For all we know she left the sect when she left the States.'

'It's possible, I suppose, but I consider it most unlikely. One interesting snippet of information I picked up at the American Embassy this morning concerned the present whereabouts of David Elkhart. According to the FBI, he's resident in England at the moment.'

Pawson was playing the reluctant virgin, waiting for me to coax the rest of what he had to offer out of him. For somebody who was so fond of the sound of his own voice it was amazing how often he dried up just as he reached the point of what he was saying. I'd always suspected he watched too many second-rate melodramas.

'Whereabouts in England?' I enquired, giving him the line he was waiting for.

'Apparently he's living just outside a place called Wisbech. That's a small market town in Cambridgeshire. Perhaps you've heard of it.'

I nodded to show that I had. If Pawson's information was correct, and I had no reason to doubt it, this placed Elkhart only thirty miles from where Vanessa Denny had been killed. Like Pawson, I didn't believe in coincidences.

While I'd been driving up to London I'd been preparing what I'd intended to say to Pawson. On the way back I went over what Pawson had had to tell me. His visit to the American Embassy had produced far more than Elkhart's current address. Although the FBI had lost much of its interest in the Messengers of God, their agents abroad had maintained a loose watching brief. What they'd had to report did nothing to show the cult in a better light.

With most of his disciples dispersed across western Europe and the rest of the world, Elkhart had faced problems both of doctrine and organization. Many of the main planks in the sect's platform which had helped it to obtain such wide publicity in the States were peculiarly American in origin. For example, potential converts in France or the Netherlands were unlikely to be turned on by a denunciation of the American public school system. Similarly, attacks on established Churches outside the States and disruption of their services would have been a sure passport to deportation.

Consequently, Elkhart had encouraged a slight change of emphasis, shifting his attacks on the Establishment from the specific to the general. He'd been searching for a doctrine which would be internationally acceptable. Prophecies of doom had remained the cornerstone of the Messengers' belief, but it had now been backed by much vaguer denunciations of capitalism and the 'System'. Elkhart had hoped this would still appeal to the drop-out element without causing too much offence to those in authority.

Dogma had given way to expediency, and this had been especially evident in Italy and France. In these countries Elkhart had encouraged his missionaries to avoid any form of confrontation with the Catholic church. 'Kiss the Pope's ass if you have to' was one of the quotes Pawson had given me and this approach had appeared to work. The Catholic hierarchy had viewed the Messengers with indulgent, if qualified, approval. On occasions it had even offered practical help in the form of accommodation and food. This was because local priests had had little idea of what went on behind the scenes. The Messengers had started to wear two faces, one for public consumption, the other for the initiated.

On the organizational side there had been a similar change in structure. Once he was in Europe Elkhart had withdrawn from the front line. He no longer toured the various communes to boost the morale of his stormtroopers, the missionaries. Instead he'd gone into retreat, accompanied by a select band of dedicated disciples, and he'd kept in touch with the rest of the faithful through a succession of 'Instructions'. With the exception of his personal bodyguard, all his companions had one feature in common – they were all young, female and extremely nubile. Elkhart had decided to enjoy a few more of the temporal fruits of spiritual power.

According to the FBI, David Elkhart had never shared the deep religious conviction of his late brother. In their estimation he was nothing more than a cheap con-artist who had struck it rich. Judging from the information available to me I found it difficult to disagree with this assessment. In the beginning his attitude appeared to have been to grab what he could while he could and be ready to run when, inevitably, the bubble burst. All new converts had been expected to donate their wealth and possessions to the Messengers' community pool. A large proportion of this pool had soon found its way to a series of numbered bank accounts in Switzerland which were for David Elkhart's personal use.

Then, about the time of Elkhart's flirtation with the comet

Kohoutek, had come the transformation. Until this point, in the FBI's estimation, everything Elkhart had done was with his tongue in his cheek. He'd known he was a sham, and he'd suspected it was simply a question of time before his converts shared the same knowledge. It was only after the faithful had unquestioningly followed him from America that the wonderful realization had suddenly struck home. His followers really did have total faith in him and what he preached. His word really was their command. For them he was exactly what he pretended to be. In their eyes he was a prophet, a direct link between them and God.

This must have been quite a moment for Elkhart, the realization that within the sect he had absolutely total power. He could manipulate his followers as he wished. His indoctrination had been so successful that the Messengers would accept absolutely anything he said as being divinely inspired. It was at this stage that Elkhart had issued the first of his 'Instructions' to the leaders of the various scattered groups of Messengers. I hadn't seen any samples of Elkhart's literary style, but Pawson had. He said that to begin with Elkhart had been cautious, doing little more than reiterate previous doctrine. As his confidence had grown, however, his instructions had become bolder. It hadn't been long before they'd become an accurate reflection of what Elkhart had been turning into himself. The Messengers had already given him wealth and power. Now they were also giving him the opportunity to bring all his deepest sexual fantasies to the fore.

From the beginning there had been more female Messengers than male, a factor which had seemed a sound reason for Elkhart's advocacy of polygamy. Elkhart himself had had three wives, but in this the Messengers had been no different from several other religious communities. To begin with, certainly, no hint of sexual scandal had attached itself to the cult. During those early, sensitive years in the States Elkhart couldn't have afforded it. Indeed, one of his chief lines of defence against attacks on the movement had been its moral basis. At the indoctrination centres only married couples had been allowed to cohabit, while singles of either sex were strictly segregated. Elkhart might have had a few dalliances on the side, but he'd taken care to be discreet. At the time, money had taken precedence over sex.

After the move away from the States, these considerations had no longer applied. Once Elkhart had realized the full extent of his power, he'd begun to use it to satisfy his every whim. Particularly attractive converts were granted personal audiences with the so-called prophet at his retreat of the moment. If they especially pleased him, they were allowed to remain in his select band of female disciples. Otherwise they were shipped back to where they had come from to continue the missionary work of the Messengers.

This missionary work had started to change, too. As the sect had grown, so had its overheads and easy pickings were harder to come by. Although new converts were still being won, revenue wasn't flowing in at the same rate it had done in America. While individual converts had always supported themselves by begging in the streets or by the sale of religious tracts, this had done nothing to help Elkhart live in the style to which he'd become accustomed.

It hadn't taken Elkhart long to come up with the answer. He might have gathered the cream of the Messengers' female membership into his personal harem, but there were thousands of other young women who were also Messengers. Why shouldn't their charms be used to win new converts, and cash, for the movement? Gradually Elkhart's 'Instructions' had begun to take on a new sexual bias. Pre-marital sex was, like any other form of physical exercise, harmful only if it was indulged in indiscriminately and to excess. A whole series of 'Instructions' had traced the history of religious prostitution back to the Greeks and Romans. The underlying message had been clear. In the Gospel according to Elkhart, the means were justified by the end. The Messengers' task was to help others to see the light, and in achieving this they should use any weapons at their disposal.

As usual, the faithful had accepted these new directives as an indication of God's will. Emboldened by this success, Elkhart had proceeded a step further. His carnal desires were legitimized and his harem expanded by its conversion into a 'school' where attractive initiates were carefully groomed in the ways they might best please a man. Yet another refinement had been a further 'Instruction' telling Messengers who used their bodies to send detailed, written accounts of their experiences to Elkhart. Presumably this was to provide him with some spicy bedtime reading and assist in selection of recruits for his harem.

I found the overall picture a most distasteful one. Admittedly, there was nothing particularly original about Elkhart's use of religious conviction as an excuse for sexual excess and indulgence. This was something which had been going on in one form or another for thousands of years. What set Elkhart apart was his total lack of scruples. For some reason, the memory which kept recurring to me was Roberts's face as he'd described his sexual adventures with Mandy Collison – and it kept company with the memory of police photographs of the charred bodies which had been recovered from the wreckage on Hunstanton beach. These were aspects of the Messengers which hadn't been publicized in any of Elkhart's 'Instructions'. If Elkhart could be stopped, this would afford me no small measure of personal satisfaction.

CHAPTER XI

Mrs Robinson was the only woman in the hotel dining-room apart from a waitress. Despite the atrocious weather, the Le Strange had been taken over by a golfing convention, which had homed in on the course which ran along the dunes as though it was some kind of Mecca. All the snippets of conversation I picked up on the way to Kim's table concerned the guests' mutual obsession. Nobody was sparing a glance for her, despite her attempt to rise to the occasion by swapping her tweeds for a dress, one of those long, shiny affairs which had been featured in so many wartime movies. Although she had all the sex appeal of a shotputter's armpit, I found myself feeling ashamed of my behaviour the previous night. I didn't like to believe I was the complete male chauvinist.

'I was betting myself that you'd sit at one of the other tables.'

Her voice had the same gravelly rasp to it which had served Louis Armstrong so well.

'I did think about it,' I admitted. 'I have my reputation to consider.'

'I bet you have.' There was no rancour to her laugh. 'There's one thing you'll learn about me, though. I may not be pretty to look at but that doesn't stop me being a good detective. Bloody good.'

'I already appreciate that – don't forget I've read some of your reports. And, by the way, there's no need to keep up the bull dike act for my benefit. I popped into Abercrombie's while I was in London and somebody showed me a photograph of you when you're not working. When you put your mind to it, you manage to look almost feminine.'

She laughed again, genuinely amused this time. My compliment had been genuine, as well. Her tweeds were simply protective camouflage to help her to survive in a man's world.

There were other people sitting too close for us to discuss the case over dinner. We saved this for when we moved to my room afterwards, an assignation which apparently offended the sense of propriety of the waitress who brought us our coffee. I couldn't begin to imagine what she thought our relationship was, but her disapproving sniff left us in no doubt about what her opinion was. It was a reaction which delighted Mrs Robinson, and was the cause of several ribald remarks after the waitress had gone, most of them at my expense. I could hardly object to the mockery after my boorish behaviour the previous night. Besides, now I was giving her a chance I was discovering there was a lot about Mrs Robinson to admire, quite apart from her ability as a private detective.

'How did it go today?' I asked once she was prepared to be serious again.

Mrs Robinson made a face which was an answer in itself.

'It was pretty much as I expected, considering I was covering ground the police had already been over. Nobody I spoke to in Snettisham came up with a positive identification of either of the girls. One or two people thought they might recognize them but they were just trying to be helpful. I'm planning to move further afield tomorrow. I thought Hunstanton might be a good bet.'

'It's in the wrong direction,' I told her. 'If the roads are still passable in the morning, I'd suggest we head towards Wisbech.'

Over the next hour or so I gave Mrs Robinson almost everything. I might just as well have given her the lot because although I protected my sources she was perfectly capable of guessing what they were. Abercrombie's would already have run a routine check on me, and doubtless they would come up with an answer which was very close to the truth. The days when agents were shrouded in mystery were long since past.

By the time I'd finished my biography of Elkhart and the Messengers, Mrs Robinson had her question ready.

'You've given me the facts, Philis,' she said. 'How about telling me what you make of them.'

'Just about everything I know about Vanessa Denny comes from your reports, so I doubt whether my conclusions are very different from yours. Judging by the way you describe her state of mind after her mother's death, the Messengers must have exerted a strong appeal. The way Mrs Denny died could hardly be construed as the work of a God of Love.'

'And Mandy Collison came into her life at just the right

97

moment. I assume she was a Messenger.'

'I don't think there's much doubt about that. From what Mr Roberts told me, she was prepared to follow Elkhart's advice about using her body in the service of Christ. Even without her, though, we'd still have the link through the girl who followed me from Oxford. She as good as admitted that she was involved in the murders.'

'Is there any possibility of questioning her further?'

'None,' I said firmly. 'And don't ask me why, because I've no intention of telling you.'

Mrs Robinson didn't need to ask. I hadn't actually given her a sworn affidavit saying Caroline had been killed, but I'd given her the next best thing. To my mind there had been no alternative. We'd be working together, and now I had a better idea of the situation I knew it could be dangerous to allow her any illusions. Elkhart would have no more compunction about disposing of a middle-aged female detective than he'd apparently had about removing others who had been in his way.

'OK,' Mrs Robinson said thoughtfully, absent-mindedly accepting the cigarette I was offering her. 'We're both agreed that murder was committed. If Elkhart's track record is anything to go by, we shouldn't have too much difficulty in establishing a motive. That leaves us with only the one problem. Proof is going to be very hard to come by.'

'The same thought had occurred to me.'

If the FBI report was accurate, and I was sure it must be, the Messengers had left a trail of bodies behind them wherever they'd gone. There hadn't been a single mention of any successful prosecutions.

'Mr Denny isn't going to be an easy man to satisfy.' Mrs Robinson was echoing another of my thoughts. 'He'll want us to come up with some hard evidence before we hand over to the police. If I'm any judge of character, he won't be satisfied with Elkhart simply being asked to move on again. He'll want to see justice done.'

'That's his problem. We take the investigation as far as we

possibly can, then it's up to him.'

Mrs Robinson probably realized I was being less than honest with her, but she was too tactful to say so.

'There's one last point before we call it a night. You say Elkhart and friends are living at a farm outside Wisbech. What you didn't say was how they acquired it. Did they buy the property, or what?'

'Apparently they pay a nominal rent,' I told her.

'So who's the landlord?'

'I thought you'd never ask. The landlord is Alistair Brown. Perhaps the name rings a bell.'

Mrs Robinson answered my grim smile with one of her own. Obviously private detectives didn't have any more faith in coincidences than I did myself.

What we did the next day was essential without being particularly fruitful. Elkhart's headquarters of the moment was on the King's Lynn side of Wisbech, just through the village of Walpole Highway. It was a big, rectangular house, set well back from the A47, which had been built at the end of the last century. I found its functional, bleak architecture appropriate to its surroundings, because the Fens could stake a very good claim to being one of the last places God had made. He'd certainly run out of hills and valleys and all the other things which made a landscape interesting. Perhaps it was my imagination, but even the people seemed a product of their environment; short, squat and weathered by the constant wind. Whatever the farmers and market gardeners might think, I'd never have bothered to reclaim the area from the sea.

As the farmhouse was clearly visible from the road and there was plenty of other traffic, I had no qualms about driving past three times. This wasn't the most rewarding of experiences. With a bitterly cold wind sweeping across the snow-covered fields, it wasn't the kind of weather which encouraged people into the great outdoors. There weren't even any Messengers out throwing snowballs. Although we

99

caught the odd flicker of movement through the uncurtained windows, this was all we did see.

'Well,' Mrs Robinson said. 'At least we know where Elkhart lives.'

'We do,' I agreed, 'and we have the number of one of his cars. We'll have this case cracked before we know it.'

The Chevette had been parked in the driveway. Either the Messengers had total confidence in its battery, they didn't give a damn, or they had another vehicle parked in the garage. As there were over a dozen people living in the house, the last was the alternative I fancied.

'Those shops we passed were a bit close to home.' Mrs Robinson wasn't allowing my lack of enthusiasm to put her off her job. 'The Messengers probably use them for their day-to-day needs, but I think we ought to leave them for the moment.'

'My own sentiments exactly.' I was glad to discover we saw eye to eye. 'Let's start a bit further afield and work our way inwards.'

Wisbech, which was our choice, looked as though it might be a total loss. Although it was little more than a sleepy market town, our enquiries were, of necessity, very much a hit-and-miss affair. I talked to a lot of people, leading up to the subject of Brown's farm and the Messengers, and none of them rose to the bait. After a time I began to suspect that I hadn't allowed for the insularity of such a rural area. People might know everything there was to know about their immediate neighbours, but their curiosity didn't extend very far. Five miles down the road was a different country – at least, this was what it appeared to be for those I spoke to.

When I met up with Mrs Robinson again I discovered she had no more to report than I had myself. Either the Messengers were maintaining a very low profile, or the population of Wisbech just didn't want to know. We grabbed a ploughman's lunch apiece in a pub in the centre of town, and once we'd finished I was all in favour of a move. I thought Walpole Highway was probably a much better bet. It was much smaller and a mile or two closer to the farmhouse. Somebody there was bound to have something to tell us.

'What you really mean, Philis, is that you're bored. You've been traipsing around all morning without any results, so you want to call it a day. You're too impatient.'

What she'd said was too accurate for me to take offence. I'd already promised myself that as soon as the rest of Abercrombie's team arrived I'd be avoiding the routine work like the plague.

'I may be impatient,' I agreed, 'but we seem to have covered most of the likely places here in Wisbech. I'm right out of ideas. I can't think of anything else here that Walpole Highway wouldn't have.'

'That's your lack of experience showing, Philis.' Mrs Robinson wasn't being unkind. She was simply stating a fact. 'We've only started to scratch the surface. I want to cover the hairdressers this afternoon. There are at least a dozen women in that house, and they'd want to keep themselves pretty for Elkhart. That will still leave me the chemists and doctors.'

'What about me?' I asked. 'What do you want me to do?'

For answer, Mrs Robinson pointed out of the pub window. Billboards were plastered all over the front of the building opposite.

'Estate agents,' I said intelligently.

'Precisely. We've been driving past For Sale signs all day.'

Although the prospect didn't fire me with enthusiasm, Mrs Robinson was the expert. As she pointed out, it was part of the estate agent's stock-in-trade to keep his ear close to the ground.

Half an hour after we'd split up again my respect for Mrs Robinson's professional competence had gone up another notch. The first estate agent on my list was a complete waste of time. He didn't respond positively to any of the photographs I showed him, and however much he knew about other people's business, he wasn't interested in sharing that knowledge with me. All that concerned him was selling houses. However, I had a feeling in my bones that my luck was about to change even before I stepped into the second office. It was a presentiment which had nothing at all to do with intuition. One of the properties for sale on display in the window was a house I knew. So did Brown and Elkhart, because closer, more careful scrutiny convinced me that my eyes hadn't been playing tricks. If anybody fancied a draughty Victorian farmhouse in the Fens, Hopkin, Willoughby and Pierce were prepared to sell it to them for £40,000 or nearest offer.

The whys and wherefores didn't interest me immediately. I hadn't noticed any For Sale sign at the farmhouse, but this wasn't important. The picture in the window meant I could try a more direct approach than the one I'd been using previously. This was why the young woman who accosted me when I first went in wasn't good enough. It didn't matter that the man I talked to was neither Hopkin, Willoughby or Pierce. Provided he was the man in charge, Leadbetter could call himself what the hell he liked.

'I represent a Mr Denny,' I told him, 'a Mr Simon Denny. You may have heard of him.'

It took a minute for Leadbetter to make the right connection. Then his eyes lit up like a winning line on a fruit-machine.

'You mean the financier?'

'The same. He's authorized me to act on his behalf in the purchase of a small property in this area. At the moment I'm obviously only at a preliminary stage, but, if the photograph is anything to go by, one of the properties you're advertising in the window seems to meet most of the specifications Mr Denny gave me.'

If Leadbetter's hopes had rocketed sky-high when I'd mentioned Denny's name they plummeted back to the ground as soon as I told him my choice. He was obviously speaking with total sincerity when he regretted that the farmhouse was no longer on the market.

'So it's already been sold?'

102

'Not quite.' Perhaps I was reading too much into Leadbetter's laugh, but he sounded as though he'd never expected to shift the farmhouse easily. The 'Or Nearest Offer' suggested that people hadn't exactly been queuing up for it. 'Mr Brown changed his mind and withdrew it from the market.'

I didn't have to do a great deal of prodding to obtain the rest of the story, what little there was of it. The only new piece of information was that Brown had known Elkhart before he'd arrived in East Anglia. According to what he'd told Leadbetter, the two of them had first met while Brown had been on holiday in Morocco the previous year.

This was interesting, but I found what the estate agent didn't tell me far more significant. I wouldn't have expected him to retail any scandal about a house he still probably hoped to sell, and he didn't. All the same, he appeared to speak of Brown's tenants with genuine respect. No mention was made of the title 'Messengers of God'. As far as Leadbetter was concerned they were an experimental religious community.

While this wasn't much of a reward for a cold day's work, at least it was an improvement on the nothing I'd had before. It also gave me another useful starting point for the night's work ahead, work which was far more to my taste.

As Laura had done the cooking the previous time we met, it was my turn to play host, and we ate at the Golden Lion. It wasn't until coffee had been served that I broached the subject of Alistair Brown. Laura had no reservations about letting me know how delighted she was by the change of subject.

'Alistair is such a bloody bore,' she said. 'Do we have to talk about him?'

'It is a part of my job,' I pointed out.

'Do I come under the heading of work, then? I thought I'd been asked out for myself alone.'

Laura was leaning slightly forward with her head resting on one hand. As she was well aware, this was a pose which

103

emphasized the shape of her full breasts. I pretended I hadn't noticed.

'I'm sorry to bore you,' I told her, 'but I really do need to find out all I can about Brown. Once business is out of the way I'll be able to concentrate exclusively on you.'

'You should see Alistair himself. He always has been his favourite topic of conversation.'

'I'd still prefer to hear your opinions first. They're likely to be more objective.'

'You're forgetting one thing, Philis.' Laura flashed me a wicked smile to show she wasn't serious. 'Alistair is supposed to be a friend of mine. I'd be betraying confidences.'

'And that would worry you?'

We both knew it didn't.

'That all depends. You see, people can change a lot in five years, Philis. Before I started talking about my acquaintances behind their backs I'd have to be sure you're still the man I used to know.'

'How exactly do you manage that?'

I didn't see any reason why I shouldn't play along with Laura. It promised to be the kind of game I'd always enjoyed.

'Can't you guess, Philis? I mean, for a start finding would obviously involve re-establishing a greater degree of intimacy.'

'Oh well,' I sighed, draining the rest of my coffee. 'I suppose everybody has to make sacrifices.'

If Denny ever came to hear of it, I hoped he would appreciate the lengths I was prepared to go to for him. I was absolutely positive I would.

It was in the small hours when I decided I had to make the effort while I could still call my mind my own. Everything else had already been mortgaged to Laura.

'Enough, woman,' I said weakly. 'Desist.'

'I thought that line was reserved for coy young maidens.'

Laura had propped herself up on one elbow.

'Coy young maidens and old men like me who are getting past it. Light me a cigarette, will you? I don't think my hands are steady enough.'

She laughed at the back of her throat and lit a couple of cigarettes. While we smoked I half-heartedly questioned her about Alistair Brown. Although Laura's answers were probably slightly distorted by personal prejudice, she did a lot to help me understand what made the farmer tick. As I'd already guessed, Brown had been born with a silver spoon in his mouth, the son of one of the wealthiest farmers in East Anglia. He was an only son, and when his parents had died he'd inherited the lot. One of the things he'd inherited had been the role of local squire, a status he took very seriously. According to Laura, he still carried far more weight than the local rural council. No motion or proposal stood any hope of success unless it had Brown's backing.

'But what's Brown like as a man?' I asked. Laura's reaction was immediate.

'He's a pompous prick.'

'I've found that out for myself. Can't you be a little more specific?'

'Well, it's only my personal opinion, but I'd classify him as some kind of sexual cripple.'

'You mean he's impotent?'

Laura's laugh showed I'd jumped to the wrong conclusion.

'He's certainly not that. What I meant was, Alistair doesn't like to play in his own league. As far as I can gather, it's something to do with his mother. From what I've heard she ruled the household with a rod of iron and still had poor Alistair tied to her apron strings when he should have been out learning a few of the facts of life. Apparently the last few generations of Browns have been a bit strange. They're one of those old inbred Norfolk families. As they've always had money, they're called eccentrics. If they'd been poor, they'd be perverts.'

'So what turns Alistair on?'

'Little girls.'

Laura's answer was succinct.

'How little is little?'

'He's not a child molester, if that's what you're thinking. Alistair is too careful for that. He makes sure his playmates are over sixteen, but he prefers to acquire them intact. So long as they're not too shop-soiled he'll accept them as old as twenty-one or twenty-two. Any woman older than that he considers a reincarnation of his mother.'

A thought had occurred to me. It probably didn't apply, but it had to be checked all the same.

'That isn't just sour grapes, is it?' I asked.

'Not likely.' Laura appeared to find the suggestion amusing. 'I scare the pants off him, and that's the way I want it to stay. I know for a fact that Alistair has had to pay off at least two sets of parents who objected to what he was doing with their daughters.'

At this point I became distracted. Laura was beginning to find the conversation boring, and now she'd finished her cigarette she'd had to think of something else to keep her hands busy. What she was doing was both unusual and vaguely titillating. Even so, she was wasting her time.

'You're flogging a dead horse,' I told her.

'Don't sell yourself short, Philis. Let's just make sure first, shall we?'

It wasn't only cars which could be supercharged. After a few seconds of tuning and priming and delicate manipulation, the dead horse had demonstrably revived. This was the main reason I didn't learn anything else about Alistair Brown until we had breakfast the next morning.

CHAPTER XII

'Christ, Philis,' Mrs Robinson said, favouring me with a lop-sided grin. 'You look like something the cat sicked up.'

If I'd been in the mood I could have pointed out that the tweeds she was modelling hardly qualified her for a spread in Vogue, but I found it difficult to disagree with her observation. I'd already seen myself in a mirror. Although being unshaven didn't help, removing the stubble wouldn't do anything about the puffiness under my eyes.

'I'm never at my best in the mornings,' I told her.

'And some mornings are worse than others. Does last night go down on expenses?'

This was a question I chose to ignore.

'Has the rest of the Abercrombie's workforce arrived yet?' I asked.

'Four of them drifted in last night,' Mrs Robinson answered. 'The other two should be here some time today.'

'Fine. In that case, I'll leave the routine work to you.'

'You're the boss. Besides, I can't imagine you being much use to anybody in your condition.'

Whatever Mrs Robinson might have thought, I'd no intention of spending the day with my feet up. Perhaps I was being defeatist, but I didn't think routine was going to take us very far. We'd established a connection between Brown and Elkhart. We could almost certainly link Vanessa Denny to Elkhart as well; then we were likely to stick. Although we might dig up enough circumstantial evidence to rekindle police interest, this was a long, long step from proving that murder had been committed. I intended to discover what would happen when I started stirring up the mud.

After Mrs Robinson had gone, I bathed, shaved and changed, then drove the nine miles to Dersingham. A Porsche and a Range Rover were standing outside Brown's house, parked beside the tennis court, something which suggested Brown might be at home. However, when I'd rung the bell, it was a woman who answered the door. A very young woman, who had long blonde hair which hung below the waistband of her jeans.

'Yes?'

The single word was sufficient to expose an accent which was unmistakably Scandinavian.

'Is Mr Brown at home?'

'No.'

There was no explanation.

'In that case, do you happen to know where I can find him?'

'No. He did not tell me.'

She wasn't trying to be rude, otherwise she wouldn't have been charming me with a big, friendly smile. She simply didn't have the vocabulary to maintain a less stilted conversation. At least, that's what I guessed.

'Do you know when he'll be back?'

'Yes.' She seemed pleased to discover she could at last say something helpful. 'Alistair said he would return at twelve o'clock. We are going out.'

This left me with another twenty-five minutes to kill. I decided I'd rather spend them inside the farmhouse than out in the car.

'Can I wait inside the house?' I asked. 'It's important I see him as soon as possible.'

'I do not think so.'

A frown had replaced her smile, but I didn't leave, because I'd just made another guess. If it was wrong, no harm would be done. If it was correct, I could be on to a winning streak.

'Tell me something,' I said. 'Are you a Messenger of God as well?'

'Yes, I am. How did you know?'

The smile had come back at increased voltage.

'It was a guess,' I admitted. 'I knew that Mr Brown was letting the Messengers use a house of his.'

'That is why I am here. The Reverend David asked me in person.'

Although she spoke with evident pride, it took me a second or two to realize that she'd been referring to Elkhart. From there on it was easy to earn my invitation into the farmhouse. While I didn't tell her any outright lies, I didn't dissuade Britta from any of the conclusions she jumped to. At first it didn't appear as though this would gain me very much apart from an opportunity to warm my feet in front of the log fire. Britta preferred smiling to talking, and I couldn't afford to be too direct with my questions. Stilted, over-grammatical English didn't mean the young Swedish girl was a fool. For most of the time we talked in generalities, circling around the areas which interested me most. The nearest I came to obtaining any pertinent information was when I asked Britta if she'd known Brown for long.

'It was two weeks ago,' she said, shaking her head. 'The Reverend David introduced us.'

'Of course. I understand that Mr Brown has done a lot to help the Messengers.'

'That is why I am here.'

By now I was convinced that Britta's English teacher's report would have mentioned something about her having the vocabulary, but lacking the confidence to string the words together. I was finding her literal, unamplified replies rather frustrating.

'Do you and Mr Brown hit it off together? You certainly seem to be at home here.'

'I suppose.' Britta accompanied this enigmatic answer with an indifferent shrug. 'I am leaving soon.'

'You're going back to Sweden?'

'No. I go back to the Reverend David.'

Every time Elkhart was mentioned her whole face lit up. I might have him down as a charlatan, con-man and murderer, but Britta obviously saw him in a completely different light. For the moment, though, Elkhart wasn't my primary concern.

'So Mr Brown will be all on his own again,' I said.

'Oh no.' Britta seemed surprised by the notion. 'It will be another girl's turn.'

This was a most unfortunate point for Brown to return. As soon as she heard the back door slam, Britta excused herself, and I doubted whether I'd ever have another chance at her. She was so ingenuous that she was bound to report our conversation verbatim to the first person who asked, and I was positive Brown would be asking. My one consolation was that although Britta and I hadn't covered much new ground, everything the Swedish girl had said had corroborated what I'd learned previously. It seemed as if prejudice hadn't coloured what Laura had told me.

Brown couldn't have been pleased to hear about his unexpected guest. He certainly wasn't in any rush to bid me welcome, because it was almost five minutes before he joined me. When he did, the veneer of civility was very thin.

'I didn't expect to be seeing you again,' he began. 'I thought we'd covered everything there was to discuss.'

'So did I at the time,' I told him. 'Since then one or two points have cropped up which need clarification.'

'I fail to see how they can possibly affect me. As far as I'm concerned, my car was stolen and it ended up at the bottom of Hunstanton cliffs.'

'With two dead bodies inside it,' I reminded. 'That's what concerns my company. We want to know exactly how and why they became dead. It seems possible that they may have been murdered.'

The silence which followed was an uneasy one as far as Brown was concerned. A lot of the wind had suddenly been removed from Brown's sails, and some time in the near future I intended to discover exactly why he was so surprised.

'I thought that the police had already established it was an accident.' He was choosing his words more carefully now. 'In any case, I don't see how I can help. I didn't know either of the girls.'

'So you said before.' I allowed enough scepticism through

110

to bring an angry flush to Brown's cheeks. 'However, that isn't what I wanted to talk to you about. I understand you own another house apart from this one, out towards Wisbech. According to the information I've received, you let it to a Mr David Elkhart. He's . . . '

'My business arrangements are none of your damn business.'

Although Brown was genuinely angry, this wasn't the reason he'd interrupted me. His was the kind of anger which was born of fear.

'I agree. What I was trying to say was . . . '

'I doubt whether I'll be interested in anything you have to say, Mr Philis. I'm a busy man, and you've already wasted more than enough of my time.'

This was the line he used to walk out on me, leaving me alone in the room. However, I did have the satisfaction of knowing he was shaken; very badly shaken, unless I was mistaken. Before I left I scrawled a brief note and propped it in a prominent position on the mantelpiece, telling Brown where he could contact me if he should reconsider. He wouldn't, of course, but I would definitely be contacting him again. When I did, Brown was going to give me some straight answers, regardless of whether he wanted to or not.

It wasn't until I reached the end of Brown's drive that I finally decided where I was going next. Even so, I wasn't being impulsive. As I'd told Denny when he'd first offered me the job, I was no investigator. The painstaking accumulation of evidence, fact by fact, bored the pants off me. I didn't have the training, the patience or the interest. Pawson used me as a blunt instrument, and blunt instruments were only effective where there was an element of confrontation. This was one very good reason for driving towards Wisbech.

There was, of course, another, more important consideration. In my own mind I was absolutely positive that both Elkhart and Brown had played a part in the death of the two girls. I wasn't a judge or jury, so the lack of hard evidence was totally immaterial. In any case, I'd already decided that Mrs Robinson was perfectly capable of uncovering any clues which might be lying around. Now I'd started pushing I had to maintain momentum. I had to continue applying pressure until something gave. Brown had been pinpointed as one weak point, and I hoped to find more at Elkhart's end. At the very least I'd be able to worry him. I might even worry him sufficiently for him to do something rash.

When I pulled up in front of Elkhart's home-from-home I expected a response of some kind. If I'd been in his situation I certainly wouldn't have welcomed casual visitors, but there was no visible reaction to my arrival. I couldn't even spot any curious faces peering out of windows. Nor did I have much more luck when I rang the doorbell. I could have been forgiven for thinking the house was deserted.

It was cold standing on the front doorstep, and the door was unlocked, a combination which decided me to invite myself inside. Although I made a point of banging the door closed, there was still no reaction from the occupants of the house, and the hairs on the back of my neck were doing their best to stand on end. My brain didn't like the conflicting data which was being fed into it. One set of senses was maintaining with great conviction that there were other people in the house. Another was pointing out the total lack of any of the normal indications of human habitation.

'Hello,' I shouted, my voice reverberating in the empty entrance hall. 'Is anybody at home?'

If they were, they weren't answering, so I tried opening a few doors. My first two selections revealed nothing more exciting than a kitchen and a study. Both rooms were empty, although they did show signs of recent occupation. However, the third door was the one I'd been looking for.

All told, there were fifteen people in the main living-room, three men and ten women. The other two had their backs to me, and it was impossible to distinguish their sex. Fourteen of them were sitting cross-legged on the floor, heads bowed, hands neatly folded in their laps. The fifteenth, David

Elkhart, was perched on a table at the far end of the room, seated in the same posture. As far as I could tell he was the only one to acknowledge my presence. At least, I thought he took a quick peek at me between slitted lids, but he was too far away for me to be absolutely sure. None of the others so much as moved a muscle.

I gently closed the door again and left them to their daily meditation or whatever. It was only slightly warmer in the entrance hall than it had been outside, and I wasn't tempted to linger. I needed some exercise to keep my blood circulating, and the form I chose was to run quietly upstairs. Of necessity, my sweep through the bedrooms had to be a quick one. Conditions were spartan, and I didn't notice much out of the ordinary apart from the religious texts which were plastered over most of the available wall space. None of them made for particularly cheerful reading, and 'THE WICKED SHALL BE TURNED INTO HELL' motif was a clear favourite.

The only bedroom which didn't display any doom-filled slogans was the one which presumably housed Elkhart himself. It was dominated by an enormous circular bed, so big that I couldn't imagine how it had been brought through the door. An equally large mirror had been set into the ceiling above it. When you threw in the red and black drapery and linen, it looked as though the furnishings had been transported direct from a second-rate brothel. So did some of the equipment I found concealed in one of the built-in cupboards. It was the kind of collection which might have been assembled by a composite of the Marquis de Sade and Xaviera Hollander.

There were a couple of locked drawers in the wardrobe which I'd have liked an opportunity to investigate, but there was the sound of movement from downstairs, a sign that meditation was over. By the time I reached the head of the stairs, Elkhart's disciples were streaming out of the room where they'd been closeted. Two of them, both male, had gained a head start on the others and were half-way up the stairs. They were big, dark and husky, bearing the unmistakable mark of the street on them. When I'd spotted them in meditation I'd immediately placed them as part of the Messengers' muscle. I could see no reason to change my opinion now. As soon as they saw me coming they stopped, effectively blocking the stairs.

'What the hell do you think you're doing?' the bigger of the two demanded.

There was no mistaking his belligerence.

'Just poking around,' I told him.

I started down towards them, and at the last moment they decided to move back to allow me through. I brushed past and continued my descent of the stairs, aware that they'd turned to follow me. My self-assurance had un-settled them, and I'd crossed the hall to the room where I'd seen Elkhart before they'd resolved their uncertainty. Although the rest of the faithful had departed, Elkhart was still squatting on the table. I propped myself against the wall by the door and lit a cigarette.

'The Reverend David doesn't like tobacco,' one of the bodyguards said from the doorway.

'Don't worry,' I told him. 'I wasn't thinking of offering him one.'

By now the bodyguards were more uncertain than ever. Although they didn't appreciate my lack of respect any more than they'd appreciated the way I'd made myself at home in their headquarters, they didn't know what to do. They were waiting upon their master's voice. I doubted whether they even broke wind unless their spiritual leader gave them the nod.

For the moment Elkhart wasn't doing anything apart from trying his damnedest to look holy and spiritual. He wasn't making a bad job of it either. Most people would have looked absurd squatting in the middle of a bloody great table but he managed to look quite impressive. It was something I'd expected after reading the FBI report. However, the section dealing with Elkhart himself had been one of the least satisfactory because leadership wasn't a quality which could be captured in words. No description of Adolf Hitler could adequately explain why tens of millions of Germans had been prepared to follow him to the very brink of hell. His appeal only became apparent when you studied the newsreels.

The same went for Elkhart. Although the FBI had stressed the part he'd played in getting the Messengers off the ground, larding the account with plenty of phrases like 'personal charisma', it was only now that I began to understand. Elkhart had presence, even on a table. Part of it had to be connected with his size because he was a big man, far bigger than the bare personal statistics had suggested. With his full beard and long hair he looked like a cross between Demis Roussos and what I imagined Rasputin must have looked like, but there was much more to him than this alone. I'd met plenty of big men, some of them with beards and long hair, and most of them had been nonentities. Elkhart had that indefinable quality which set some men apart and it was impossible to miss. Even his total immobility suggested some inner power and if he could impress an old cynic like me, it was hardly surprising he'd had such an effect on the young.

'Most impressive,' I said, 'but I'd come down now. If you stay like that much longer, your knees are likely to lock.'

Elkhart was in no particular hurry to answer me. It was a full minute before he raised his head to look at me. As soon as he opened his eyes a part of his appeal became apparent. On a woman they would have been beautiful. On Elkhart they were striking, with large, very green irises surrounded by very clear whites. Even if he was using drops, this didn't detract from their slightly mesmeric effect, a quality which was enhanced by his ability to maintain an unblinking stare. When he spoke I immediately recognized the second major weapon in his armoury. There was a rich resonance to his deep voice which must have been ideally suited to both the pulpit and the boudoir.

'You must be Mr Philis,' he said.

'That's right. I'm glad your friend Brown has paved the way for me.'

Although I hadn't anticipated Elkhart's approach, it hadn't taken me as much by surprise as he'd probably hoped. I'd assumed that Brown would be in contact with him. Indeed, I was rather gratified by the development. Brown must have been more disturbed by my visit than I'd thought if he'd telephoned Elkhart so soon.

'That wasn't quite what he did.' Elkhart drew attention to his voice by talking slowly and with great deliberation. 'Alistair warned me about you. He said you were a trouble-maker.'

'He's prejudiced. He found the questions I was asking difficult to answer.'

'He told me you had a problem with your attitude. Now I can see what he meant.'

I could understand exactly what Elkhart was trying to do. If he didn't allow me an opportunity to ask any questions, he wouldn't be forced to tell me any lies. I was also scheduled for the bum's rush at any second. I did my best to forestall Elkhart by bringing out the photographs from my inside pocket. They'd had a lot of wear over the past couple of days.

'Vanessa Denny and Mandy Collison,' I said, holding out the snapshots to him. 'I believe you knew both of them.'

Elkhart didn't even spare the photographs a glance.

'Mr Philis, it's time you left,' he answered. 'Carl, Steven, see him out.'

Carl and Steven obviously liked the idea. They took an arm apiece and I offered no resistance when they ma-noeuvred me towards the door. Elkhart wasn't going to say anything even if I stayed; and I didn't feel like fighting. On the other hand I didn't feel like being roughed up either. When we reached the front door I applied the brakes, bringing the two bodyguards to a halt beside me.

'I'm a big boy now,' I told them. 'I can manage the rest of the way under my own steam.'

'But we enjoy helping people,' Carl or Steven said.

116

'Sure,' Carl or Steven agreed. 'It makes us feel good.'

'I'll just bet it does.' By now I was beginning to be irritated. 'Neither of you will be feeling very good, though, unless you let go of my arms. You may be the bully-boys around Elkhart's private harem, but where I come from you wouldn't rate at all.'

Although I could probably have persuaded them on my own, Elkhart had been following behind us and he decided to lend me a hand.

'Let him go, boys,' he instructed. 'There's no need to be rough. Goodbye, Mr Philis.'

I waited until Carl and Steven had obeyed orders before I turned around.

'Why not make it *au revoir*,' I suggested, 'because I shall be back. Before I go, though, I'll give you another name to think about. Don't you ever wonder what happened to Caroline Winters?'

It was a good exit line, and I was feeling quite pleased with myself as I climbed into my car. My complacency lasted until I'd almost reached the road. It was effectively destroyed when Laura drove past me, heading for where Elkhart and his bodyguards were still standing in the open doorway.

CHAPTER XIII

'You're crazy, Philis.'

Mrs Robinson delivered her judgement with total conviction. Indignation had been battling with incredulity all the while I'd been explaining what I'd done with my day.

'Maybe,' I conceded, slightly on the defensive, 'but I'd call it a calculated risk. In any case, it won't interfere with what you and your colleagues are doing.'

'Like hell it won't.' My attempt to placate Mrs Robinson was a miserable failure. 'You do realize what Elkhart is going to do, don't you?'

117

'I think I have a fair idea, yes.'

I was wasting my breath. Mrs Robinson was building up an impressive head of steam and it had to be released no matter what I said.

'Elkhart is going to pull out,' she forged on angrily. 'He's going to pack his bags and move on, just like he has done every other time he's been in trouble. Where will that leave our investigation then?'

'In great difficulty,' I admitted, 'but it isn't going to happen like that. Even if he was the type, Elkhart doesn't have any reason to panic.'

Although Mrs Robinson wasn't an easy woman to convince, I had the advantage of having foreseen most of her objections. Even where I was justifying what I'd done in retrospect, I had a strong case to put. One of my most compelling arguments was historical. Ever since David Elkhart had assumed command, mysterious deaths among the Messengers' ranks had been a regular occurrence. Most of them had taken place in the United States, but there had been several others scattered across Europe and North Africa. Even where these deaths had demonstrably been murders, and suspicion had fallen upon the Messengers, there hadn't been one single instance of a successful prosecution. In every case the pattern had been the same. No matter that the evidence had pointed in their direction, it had always been circumstantial, and suspicion was a long step away from proven guilt. I couldn't see that the deaths of Vanessa Denny and Mandy Collison were substantially different.

This, of course, was a direct affront to Mrs Robinson's professional pride, and to begin with she'd objected vehemently. However, she was realistic enough for her objections soon to lose most of their sting. As I kept on emphasizing, our viewpoint was distorted. We both knew Elkhart had had the two girls killed, but we didn't have a shred of proof to back us up. Although we could probably prove Brown was lying, and we could certainly link the girls with the Messengers, this was the most we could do. Even if we did manage to dig up more there was little or nothing we could do about the biggest stumbling block of all. There were any number of Messengers who would do anything, up to and including a life sentence in prison, to protect their leader, and Elkhart was the man we were gunning for. To settle for anything less would be tantamount to an admission of failure.

Once Mrs Robinson had accepted this she could see why Elkhart wasn't likely to run. He was as well aware of the realities of his situation as we were ourselves. Although he'd been forced to move on before, he'd been responding to very different kinds of pressure. In the States he'd had little difficulty in weathering all the legal storms which had begun with the shooting of his brother. He'd eventually left because of an attack on his financial base, not on his person. Again, in Morocco, there had been a different kind of pressure. He'd known he was facing an autocratic regime which wasn't necessarily bound by such luxuries as proof and evidence.

His present position was far less precarious. The official enquiry hadn't even turned up his name, while my own unofficial efforts wouldn't cause him to lose too much sleep. He knew as well as I did that I was doing little more than scratch the surface.

'OK,' Mrs Robinson conceded grudgingly. 'You've made your point. What you're saying is that I'm wasting my time. Nothing I do is going to take us any closer to Elkhart.'

'That isn't what I'm saying at all.' Now Mrs Robinson had swung too far towards the opposite extreme. 'What I'm suggesting is a two-pronged attack. I'll keep on stirring the pot to see what surfaces, but the bread-and-butter work is equally important. Denny isn't going to be satisfied with suppositions. The more you can dig up which connects Vanessa with Elkhart the better.'

'Since you brought the subject up, what about Mr Denny? Are you keeping him up to date with what we're doing?'

I shook my head.

'He hasn't asked for progress reports, and until he does I'm not giving him one. Anyway, to date we don't really have a great deal to tell him.'

By now we'd covered all the relevant points bar one, and Mrs Robinson was astute enough to realize what it was I'd overlooked. It was something I'd have had to bring up anyway, but Mrs Robinson provided me with a tailor-made introduction.

'You know, Philis,' she said, 'Elkhart isn't simply going to sit back and do nothing. Everything we know about the man indicates that he tends to over-react to provocation. You maintain that he won't run, and I'm inclined to agree with you. On the other hand, Elkhart has already patented a sure-fire method of dealing with nuisances. Unless he's suddenly mellowed he's likely to start thinking in terms of arranging an accident for you.'

'That does seem to be a distinct possibility,' I concurred.

There wasn't very much point in pretending to be surprised by this endorsement of my own assessment of Elkhart, so I gave her a more detailed account of the previous attempt on my life. Once again Mrs Robinson was quick to grasp the implications of what I was saying.

'You really are crazy, Philis.' She was shaking her head in disbelief. 'Why don't you go the whole hog and send that maniac a written invitation to kill you?'

'It would clarify our doubts about Elkhart if he did try, wouldn't it? And, in case you're wondering, I don't have a death wish. I shall be watching my back very carefully.'

The expression on Mrs Robinson's face suggested I hadn't said anything to change her opinion of my state of mind.

'You're the boss,' she said, 'but rather you than me.'

'Exactly. That's why I've booked you out of here in the morning and reserved a room in your name at the Golden Lion in Hunstanton. If Elkhart does turn nasty, I don't want you too closely associated with me.'

Mrs Robinson didn't argue at all. She didn't say as much, but I suspected she wanted to be as far away from me as possible.

*

The one factor I hadn't mentioned to Mrs Robinson concerned Laura. It was something which had been worrying me ever since she'd driven past me earlier in the day. Although it had been an unexpected development, I suspected it was one which could have been avoided if I'd had the sense to put my foot down. I'd learned all about Laura's impetuosity a long time before and what I'd had to say about the Messengers had obviously intrigued her. She'd also made it perfectly clear that she was eager to help me in any way she could. God alone knew what she thought she could do at Elkhart's headquarters but feminine curiosity must have clouded her better judgement and she could always justify herself by saying I hadn't categorically refused her assistance. This was the only possible reason I could think of for Laura walking straight into the lion's den.

For all I knew she'd walked straight out again, but, if she had, Laura certainly hadn't returned home. I'd made two attempts to telephone her at the cottage before I spoke to Mrs Robinson and there had been no reply on either occasion. Although this didn't prove anything I had good reason to be concerned for her safety. Elkhart would want to know as much about me as possible after my visit, and Alistair Brown would be his major source of information. As Brown and Laura moved in the same circles there was a distinct possibility he was already aware of our relationship. I hoped I was worrying unnecessarily, but I had an unpleasant premonition that I wasn't.

Laura and I had arranged to meet at the Le Strange at eight o'clock, and I made due allowance for the female prerogative to be late. By half past the hour I'd allowed Laura all the prerogative she was going to have and tried to ring the cottage again. There was still no reply. My last faint hope lay in Reception, where I drew yet another blank – there had been no messages for me at all. I no longer expected there to be one, but I left Laura's home number at the desk just in case. The young receptionist promised to contact me there if anything did turn up.

There were no lights shining behind any of the windows of the cottage. Nor was there any note pinned to the door to explain why she hadn't kept our date. Although I hadn't expected to find anything, it was something I'd had to check. While I was there I decided to take a quick look inside the cottage. The lock didn't detain me long and I spent almost half an hour going through the various rooms without finding a single thing which might explain Laura's visit to Elkhart. When I'd finished my rudimentary search I rang through to the Le Strange where there were no messages for me. By now I considered myself to have done my duty. I'd gone through all the motions without any reward, and I felt I was entitled to stop pussyfooting around. Instead of trying to discover why Laura had gone to see Elkhart, it was high time I went to fetch her back.

Before I left the cottage I smoked a cigarette and went over all the reasons why it wasn't worth contacting the police. There was nothing to prevent me telephoning them to say that I suspected a Mrs Laura Cunningham was being held against her will at a farmhouse on the Wisbech road, but the drawbacks were obvious. Even if this hadn't been mere supposition on my part, a lengthy explanation would be necessary to stir the police into action, and there was nothing I could say which would merit a full-scale raid. The best I could hope for would be a couple of polite local bobbies knocking at the front door, and, if I was any judge of Elkhart, they wouldn't find anything to merit further investigation.

In any case, I didn't want to involve the police, which was the best reason of all. The roads were free of everything except slush and ice and I managed the twenty-odd miles in even time, something which didn't do a great deal for my nerves. I just wasn't a good enough driver to cope with that speed in the prevailing conditions.

The first step was for me to establish Laura's presence, and there was no sign of her TR7 outside the farmhouse when I

122

drove slowly past. There was a big lay-by a quarter of a mile up the road and I left my car there, trudging back towards the farmhouse through the deep snow piled at the side of the road. It wasn't only my feet which became cold from the snow falling into my shoes. The usual icy wind was blasting across the Fens and the left-hand side of my face felt as though it had frozen solid by the time I reached the gate at the end of the drive.

For the moment I didn't particularly want anybody to know I was there. In the morning the tracks I made ploughing through the undisturbed snow of the shrubbery would be glaringly apparent but by the morning this would no longer matter. A little more melted slush in my shoes seemed infinitely preferable to marching in plain view down the centre of the driveway.

There were two vehicles standing outside the farmhouse, the Chevette and an old Dormobile. The vehicles inside the garage were obscured by the frosted glass of the small windows. Although the main sliding doors were probably unlocked they didn't appeal to me at all. In my experience, sliding doors usually made a hell of a lot of noise. The small door of the garage struck me as being a far better bet. It was locked, but my Diners' Club card won its customary victory over Yale.

One quick glimpse of Laura's TR7 parked beside a second Dormobile was all that I needed. I pocketed my torch, relocked the door and retraced my footsteps to the front of the house. I'd done all the undercover work I intended to do for the evening. When I rang the doorbell the response was immediate.

'Yes?' the girl asked.

She had long dark hair and a well-filled T-shirt which proclaimed 'Jesus Lives'.

'I want to see Mr Elkhart,' I told her. 'May I come in?'

'Sure,' she said, starting to open the door wider. 'I'll go and tell him you're here.'

'Hold it a minute, Marcia.'

123

The larger of Elkhart's two bodyguards had also heard the doorbell. He might not have been fast enough to prevent Marcia from answering the door, but he had no intention of allowing her to invite me inside.

'But, Carl . . . ' she began when he pushed her unceremoniously aside.

'Forget it, love. You go back to the others and I'll handle this.'

Carl's way of handling the situation was to crowd me back on the top doorstep. He didn't forget to pull the door almost closed behind him.

'I thought we'd managed to get rid of you this afternoon,' he said nastily.

'You should have listened to me. I said I'd be back. I've come to collect Mrs Cunningham.'

'Mrs Cunningham? Who the hell is she?'

Carl didn't expect me to believe him, and I didn't. However, this didn't stop me from trying to play it straight.

'She's the woman who owns the TR7 parked in your garage,' I explained patiently. 'She arrived here just as I left this afternoon.'

I had a good reason for my patience. Although I was prepared for trouble, I wasn't actively seeking it out and I didn't like the look of the three-foot length of hose Carl had in his right hand. Of course, it could be I'd interrupted him in the middle of some household chore like plumbing in a washing machine. On the other hand, it could be the hose had been packed with lead. Broken limbs and fractured skulls weren't part of the price I was ready to pay for Laura's recovery.

'Mrs Cunningham will leave when she's good and ready and not before.' Carl's smile showed how confident he was. 'She doesn't need you to hold her hand.'

'I'd far rather she told me that herself.'

As always, it happened fast, beginning when I took a step towards the door. Carl swung the weighted hose at my head in a vicious arc which would have made me an immediate candidate for an intensive care unit if it had landed, and I blocked his wrist with my forearm. He'd left himself so wide open I could have hit him anywhere, but I wasn't feeling charitable. I deliberately chose a point a few inches south of his navel and put my knee into his face when he doubled over. Cowboys like Carl had to learn to live with a little pain.

The length of hose was in my hand as I went through the door, and it appeared as though I had a ready-made target immediately. The girl who had answered the door to me was still in the entrance hall, wondering what was happening to her orderly existence, and I only spared her a fleeting glance. My attention was reserved for Steven, the second bodyguard, who had been striding purposefully towards the door. The hose and the expression on my face were all the warning he needed. He stopped where he was and held up his hands in a placatory gesture.

'OK, chief,' he said quickly. 'There's no need for any more violence.'

'I'll be the judge of that.'

The adrenalin was still flowing, and I had every intention of trampling over anybody who stood in my way.

'Sure, sure.' Although Steven was backing cautiously away he seemed more amused than apprehensive. 'Did you know you had blood on your trousers?'

'Don't worry,' I told him. 'It's not mine. Where do I find Mrs Cunningham?'

'She's upstairs. If you wait here, I'll go and fetch her for you.'

'I'm not waiting anywhere. You lead and I'll follow.'

Steven shrugged, the irritating half-smile still on his face.

'She might not want to be disturbed.'

When I slapped the weighted hose into the palm of my left hand Steven forgot all about his objections. He merely shrugged again and turned to start up the stairs. Although this was no more than I'd asked him to do, I'd have been much happier if he hadn't been smirking. There was something drastically wrong. It had all been made far too easy for

125

me. I was beginning to have the uncomfortable suspicion that I was doing precisely what Elkhart wanted of me.

'The Reverend David isn't going to like this,' Steven warned me.

'What a shame. Just do as you're told and open the door.'

Still smirking, Steven gave another of his shrugs and threw open the door, stepping back out of the way so I wouldn't miss anything. My first impression was that it wasn't only Elkhart's face and head which were hairy. A thick pelt of black hair ran from his shoulderblades to the base of his spine and covered his legs from top to bottom, leaving his bare buttocks sticking out like two pink islands. As he was on top of Laura, this was all I could see of him.

There was no possible doubt about what the two of them were doing together. Laura's arms and legs were wrapped as tightly around Elkhart as they had been around me the previous night. The small sounds of pleasure she was making at the back of her throat had the same intensity I remembered. Presumably this was what Elkhart meant when he referred to his 'missionary role'.

He allowed me a second or two to admire his technique before he pretended to become aware of his audience. As soon as he did, he withdrew, pulling the sheet up to cover his nakedness. His expression of outrage might have been contrived, but it looked perfectly genuine. Laura simply lay where she was, sprawled wantonly on her back, and made no effort to hide her body. It was impossible to guess what she was thinking, but whatever it was I could see in her eyes, I didn't like it.

'What's going on?'

Elkhart's question hung heavily in the air, and I hoped my face didn't mirror my confusion. There was only one line to play, and I played it, acutely aware of the built-in credibility gap.

'I've come for Laura,' I said woodenly. 'I'm taking her back home.'

126

Steven sniggered from behind me. His reaction didn't do a thing to make what I'd said any more impressive.

'Are you mad, Philis?' Elkhart demanded, his tone incredulous. 'What right do you have to come bursting into my bedroom like that? Do I have to draw you diagrams, or do you realize what we were doing?'

Steven sniggered again. I promised myself that if he did it once more he'd be sniggering through a mouthful of broken teeth.

'I saw.' My voice remained as wooden as before. 'Come on, Laura. Put some clothes on and we'll leave.'

'My God.' Now it was Laura's turn and she was shaking her head in wonder. 'You're unbelievable, Philis. You're even worse than Tony, and that's saying something. One night in bed together doesn't mean you own me. I don't want to go anywhere with you. I'm enjoying myself here. At least, I was until you interrupted.'

'You heard the lady,' Elkhart put in. 'Now get off my property before I call the police.'

I ignored him completely. For the moment Elkhart was an irrelevance. I was concentrating exclusively on Laura, trying to read what might be going on in her mind.

'Listen, Laura,' I said. 'I don't know what threats have been used, but they don't apply any longer. If you want to leave, nothing is going to happen to you. I can promise you that.'

Although Laura had at last covered her nakedness we were still operating on totally different wavelengths.

'Can't you get it into your head that I've no intention of going anywhere with you.' She was speaking slowly and clearly, making sure each word sank home. 'For Christ's sake, grow up, Philis. There was never anything between us except some rather unimaginative sex, and there never will be. It doesn't give you any right to interfere in my life. Get the hell out of here and leave me in peace.'

'Is that clear enough for you?' Elkhart enquired. 'Are you going, or do I have to telephone the police?'

I went. There was nothing else I could do unless I wanted to make a bigger fool of myself than I had already. Elkhart had just wiped the floor with me, and my grudge against him had become even more personal. Putting him out of business had become a question of self-respect.

CHAPTER XIV

Back at the car I didn't drive off immediately. I preferred to start the engine, thumb the heater on to high and light myself a cigarette. There were two possible interpretations of what had taken place at the farmhouse, and neither of them redounded to my credit. The facts, such as they were, couldn't have been clearer. Indeed, they were so clear that there had been no real alternative to backing off with my tail between my legs. Earlier in the afternoon I'd been an eye-witness to Laura's arrival at Elkhart's headquarters. There had been no suggestion of any form of duress, not a solitary grain of evidence to indicate she'd been forced there against her will. Nor was there any disputing what I'd seen when I'd barged into Elkhart's bedroom. There had been no clever tricks with mirrors, and Laura had appeared to be an active, and enthusiastic, participant in the sexual frolics. She'd also been at some pains to explain how appearances weren't at all deceptive. It was a message which had come across loud and clear.

On this basis there shouldn't have been room for even a shadow of doubt in my mind. Laura had simply been satisfying that itch between her legs, an itch which had already led her into bed with me, Tony and, no doubt, hordes of other faceless men. It was time I put her out of my mind and concentrated on the important issues.

This was an interpretation I hadn't seriously considered for a moment, an attitude which had nothing to do with Laura's slur on my virility. It was probably what Elkhart would have liked me to believe but I knew from experience how easy it was to choreograph situations so that they gave a totally false impression. Besides, I knew Laura far better than Elkhart did and this was where the whole charade had fallen down. To Elkhart's eyes Laura's histrionics would have appeared perfectly satisfactory. Whatever else Brown might have been able to tell him about Laura and myself, he wouldn't have known that our relationship stretched back far further than a couple of days.

However, I had far more to work on than a simple conviction that Laura had been acting completely out of character. She might have had a temporary aberration and forgotten her training when she'd driven in to see Elkhart but she'd remembered when the pressures and threats had been brought to bear. She'd deliberately stressed our one night together when she'd been talking to me and, just to make sure, she'd then proceeded to compare me with Tony. Put together, and seen in the context of our true relationship, they were as good as a signed statement that the words she was speaking weren't her own.

I even knew how the whole thing had been set up. Skulking through the shrubbery had been fine when I thought I wasn't expected but, as Elkhart would have had people watching for me, it had been a wasted precaution. He couldn't have been sure I'd come but it would have seemed a distinct possibility, and I'd probably been spotted long before I rang the doorbell. This would have given Elkhart plenty of time to set the scene, especially if Laura had been pre-rehearsed, and Carl had simply been added insurance. His job had been to delay me long enough for the finishing touches to be made.

I'd appreciated most of this long before I left the house and only one thing had stopped me from acting there and then. Verbal threats alone would never have been sufficient to make Laura behave the way she had. After all, she knew who I was and what I did for a living. There had to have been some actual physical menace, something which had convinced her that neither of us would leave the house alive unless she cooperated with Elkhart. As I'd been unable to identify this random factor, I'd had no choice other than to defer to Laura's judgement. What was happening to her might not be very pleasant but it was still a hell of sight better than me getting her killed.

This left just one other point unexplained. It would have been far simpler for Elkhart to conceal Laura somewhere I couldn't possibly find her and eliminate all traces of her presence. Alternatively, if he'd considered her a real threat, he could easily have disposed of her. Instead, he'd elected to flaunt Laura's infidelity in front of me, and making me jealous wouldn't have been his motive. I stayed with the assumption that he'd wanted to prove conclusively that Laura's presence was entirely voluntary. This in turn implied that Elkhart had a use for her, and I thought I knew just the man to help me learn what it might be. It was high time Mr Alistair Brown came down to earth to face a few of the realities of life.

It was ten o'clock when Brown left his house the following morning, driving his Range Rover and with Britta on the front seat beside him. I maintained a loose tail until Brown was safely on the road to King's Lynn, then I did a U-turn and headed back to the farm. The Swedish girl had been carrying a couple of shopping bags over her arm, so I didn't expect to be disturbed too soon.

Most farms I'd visited had been swarming with dogs, but Brown's appeared to be an exception, something for which I was duly grateful. Housebreaking loses much of its appeal when there are a couple of slavering Alsatians to fend off. Once I was safely inside and had relocked the back door I drifted aimlessly from room to room, poking into drawers and cupboards and wardrobes and anywhere else which took my fancy. I was being nosey, not really expecting to find anything, which all went to show how wrong I could be. Brown's collection of Polaroid erotica was inside one of the locked drawers I forced, concealed among a pile of bills and bank

130

statements. There were about fifty prints, most of them of poor quality, and all of them depicted young women dressed, or half-dressed, as schoolgirls. Although there were plenty of shots of navy-blue knickers and functional girlish bras there wasn't a single nude in the collection. Apart from the colour, there was almost a Victorian flavour about the photographs.

I selected a handful of the snapshots at random and took them downstairs with me when I went. After I'd shoved a few logs on the fire and helped myself to some of my host's whisky there was nothing to do except wait. Fortunately, I didn't have to wait very long. It was only a little over an hour before I heard the Range Rover outside. When I peeked out from behind the cover of the curtains I discovered that Britta was no longer with Brown. This was an unanticipated bonus. While I'd had no intention of allowing her to interfere with my plans for Brown she was a complication I was happy to do without.

By the time Brown came into the living-room I was sprawled in the armchair again, sipping whisky from my replenished glass. It was a sight which stopped Brown dead in his tracks.

'You're back sooner than I expected, Alistair,' I said, doing my best to fill in the awkward silence. 'I was afraid I might have to wait until your girl-friend had finished her shopping.'

It interested me to notice that Brown wasn't frightened yet. For the time being he was still on an Englishman's-Home kick, and outrage was his dominant emotion. He was so taken aback it took him a few seconds to decide which question should have priority.

'What the devil do you think you're doing here?' I suggested helpfully. 'That would make a good start.'

Brown had a much better idea of his own. He came out with a strangled grunt, then strode purposefully across the room to the telephone. I permitted him to dial the first 9 before I pushed myself to my feet.

'Aren't you being a trifle hasty, Alistair?' I asked

131

It wasn't the question which persuaded him to change his mind. It was the photograph I was waving under his nose. When he saw it, he did start to be frightened. The colour ebbed from his face, and he forgot all about the telephone receiver he was holding.

'Where did you get that?'

His voice was little more than a whisper.

'Surely you recognize it, Alistair?' I was using his Christian name like a goad. 'It's part of your little collection. You really are a naughty old farmer, aren't you?'

The first time I hit him I didn't clench my fist. Just the same, all my weight went behind the slap, and when Brown went down he dragged the telephone from the table with him.

'Come on,' I said. 'Back on your feet. We're only just getting started.'

To begin with Brown didn't want to play. He wanted to talk, not fight, but I wouldn't allow him to. I didn't have the inclination or patience to sort through a maze of lies and half-truths. When the questioning started I wanted honest answers straight away, and what I did to Brown was the quickest way I knew of guaranteeing satisfaction.

Neither the beating I administered nor the interlude in the bathroom were important in themselves, although I doubted whether Brown would have agreed with me. He wasn't in a position to appreciate my control and discipline. All he knew was that he was in a nightmare where I continued hurting and frightening him no matter how desperately he tried to defend himself. And I kept on hurting and frightening him long after Brown thought he'd had enough. I was teaching Brown that the normal rules governing civilized human behaviour were suspended until I decided otherwise.

According to what I'd been taught about interrogation techniques I shouldn't have stopped when I did. Now that Brown was softened up I should have pressed home my advantage. He already knew I didn't have any scruples about hurting him. Five minutes with his face near a basinful of water had suggested I was perfectly prepared to kill him if necessary. The next step should have been to demonstrate that my lack of scruples covered all the stages in between, but I didn't have the stomach for it. What I'd done already would leave a permanent scar and I wasn't interested in destroying Brown. I wanted to leave him some tattered shreds of self-respect he could reassemble once I'd finished with him.

It was almost a quarter of an hour before Brown showed any signs of moving from where he was lying curled up on the floor beside his bed. When he did, I instructed him to sit on the bed, and he didn't offer any argument. Movement might be painful but he was intelligent enough to realize the probable punishment for disobedience. He sat forward on the edge of the bed, head held in his hands, and watched the blood drip from his nose to the carpet.

'When will your girl-friend be back?' I asked.

'Britta? I'm supposed to be picking her up in King's Lynn.'

One side of Brown's face was swelling up, and he spoke with a newly-developed lisp. Although he was avoiding my eye, the prompt reply was an encouraging sign.

'Whereabouts and what time?'

'I said I'd pick her up at the Woolpack at half past two. That's a pub on the Tuesday Market place.'

'What about other engagements? Is there anybody you have to see?'

There was a slight hesitation before Brown answered. I interpreted this as another good sign. Brown wanted to make sure his reply was accurate. The very last thing he wanted was to upset me.

'I don't have any hard and fast arrangements,' he told me. 'One or two people may expect to see me, but they won't be particularly surprised if I don't show up.'

'So nobody is likely to turn up here?'

'I wouldn't have thought so.'

'For your sake, let's hope you're right.'

The threat was almost certainly gratuitous but it wasn't likely to do any harm. The same went for my phone call to the Woolpack, leaving a message for Britta to find her own way home. If I couldn't persuade Brown to tell me everything in the two hours available to me, I'd hand Pawson in my cards.

Before I asked any more questions, I surprised Brown by taking him through into the bathroom to clean up his face. I wasn't at all proud of what I'd done to him, and the blood on his face was a reproach my conscience could do without. Besides, Brown would probably find it easier to talk if he realized there was some small spark of humanity struggling for life inside me, and he'd have plenty of other aches and pains to remind him what I was capable of when provoked.

'Let me make one thing absolutely clear,' I said once we were back in the bedroom. 'All that interests me are straight answers to the questions I'm going to ask. There's no need for any more unpleasantness.'

'There was no need for it before.'

Brown wasn't being defiant. He was simply expressing a heartfelt belief. I thought it advisable to explain my attitude, and give him another warning of sorts.

'This is the third time we've met,' I pointed out. 'On both the other occasions you refused to come up with satisfactory answers. I was simply demonstrating that I'm no longer prepared to settle for anything less than the truth. I hope that's clearly understood.'

It certainly appeared to be. To begin with I made it easy for Brown by keeping my questions general. Although I wasn't particularly interested in how he'd first come into contact with the Messengers it was good practice for the more important questions which would come later. It also taught Brown that I wouldn't be satisfied with fudged answers. I wanted the entire truth, no matter how poor a light it showed him in.

What it boiled down to was that Brown had been on

134

holiday to Marrakesh the previous year, taking along his girl-friend of the moment. Apparently their relationship hadn't been durable enough to survive the change of climate, especially with a group of randy young German tourists staying at the same hotel. Within the first few days Brown's girl had moved into the room of one of the Germans and Brown had suddenly found himself on his own. The holiday had given every indication of turning into an unmitigated disaster, and Brown had seriously considered returning home on the first available plane. However, he'd soon changed his mind once he'd found himself a German of his own.

In actual fact, Berthe had found him, stopping Brown in the street and asking him for alms. Although she was by no means the first beggar Brown had encountered in Morocco, she had been by far the prettiest. As a result he'd ended up offering her far more than alms, and Berthe had had no objections. The religious instruction she'd tried to mix in with the sex was an irritant, but it had obviously been important to her, and Brown had played along. One girl was enough to lose on any holiday.

Up to this point Brown's narrative was straightforward enough. Thereafter I was obliged to do a lot of reading between the lines, because Brown had no real idea how he'd been manipulated. From what Pawson had told me, I already knew that at that time Elkhart had been living quite openly on the outskirts of Marrakesh, occupying a mansion which was the holiday home of a wealthy Californian businessman. According to Brown, it had been Berthe's idea for him to visit the commune. However, it seemed far more probable to me that Elkhart himself must have wanted to arrange the meeting. Berthe would have mentioned the rich Englishman she had in tow, and this was precisely the kind of contact Elkhart needed. He was experiencing increasing difficulties with the Moroccan authorities, and he'd have known it was only a question of time before he was forced to move his court elsewhere. Brown must have seemed like the

135

answer to a prayer.

Brown had apparently felt much the same way about Elkhart. For the last week of his holiday he'd spent more time at Elkhart's mansion than he had at his hotel, and he'd been entertained like visiting royalty. This entertainment had included access to the harem. Although Brown phrased his experiences differently, it was plain that Elkhart had summed him up pretty accurately. Brown had been encouraged to screw himself silly.

'And was this when you offered Elkhart the use of your spare farmhouse?' I asked.

'Oh no. That came later.' I'd given Brown a towel to dry his hair, and he was twisting it nervously in his hands. 'When I left Marrakesh, I'd arranged to go back there for another holiday. I was actually going to stay with David. Then he sent me a letter saying he had to leave Morocco. He said he was thinking of coming to England, and asked if I'd look around for somewhere suitable for him to stay. That's when I offered to rent him the house.'

'Is rent quite the right word?' I asked. There was no harm in Brown's knowing what I thought of him. 'Exactly what do you charge Elkhart? A woman a month?'

'It isn't like that at all.'

Even if Brown hadn't been too nervous to come up with a convincing denial I doubt whether he would have believed himself. He wasn't enjoying my research into his sexual habits much more than what had gone before. It was forcing him to face too many uncomfortable truths about himself. I applied a bit more pressure by taking his photographs from the drawer I'd forced and strewing them on the bed.

'So what are these, then?' I enquired. 'Your Schoolgirl of the Month collection? From where I'm sitting those photos look pretty sick. What was your arrangement with Elkhart?'

'There wasn't one.' Brown still sounded as though he would have liked to convince himself. 'When David first moved in there weren't enough beds for everybody. He asked me if I minded one of the girls staying here with me.'

'Of course he did,' I said. 'Which one was she?'

Brown didn't answer, and I wasn't pressing him. I'd been able to guess at the nature of the arrangement when I'd first met Britta, and the photographs merely provided me with corroboration. Apart from the Swedish girl there were several others I recognized among the collection. One of them had opened the door for me when I'd called on Elkhart the previous night, and there were at least two others I'd seen about the place. Unfortunately, neither Mandy Collison nor Vanessa Denny had posed for their portraits. Or if they had, Brown had taken care to dispose of the evidence.

'OK,' I said. 'Now tell me about the two girls who went over the cliff in your car.'

'I've told you already, and I swear it's the truth.' I could hear the desperation in Brown's voice. 'My car was stolen from the pub car park. The first I knew of the accident was when the police contacted me.'

I tended to believe Brown as far as he'd gone. I couldn't really envisage him as a murderer, or even as an active accessory come to that. He just didn't have the backbone for it. His guilt lay elsewhere.

'You must have known the victims were connected with Elkhart,' I pointed out.

'Yes.' The admission came reluctantly. 'I recognized the Collison girl. I'd seen her with David.'

'Why didn't you tell the police that?'

'I don't know.' Brown's head was back in his hands. 'I wish to God I had. I suppose I was afraid of becoming involved.'

Despite Brown's evident distress the answer came too pat, as though it had been rehearsed. All the same, I decided to let it pass for the moment. I still had to pinpoint what it was Brown was trying to conceal.

'How about the other girl?' I asked. 'You must have guessed she was one of Elkhart's protégées as well.'

Brown nodded miserably. He was becoming unhappier by the second, torn by the conflict of protecting himself on two fronts. He didn't want to implicate himself in the deaths, and he most definitely didn't want to annoy me.

'Come on, Brown.' I allowed my impatience to show. 'You knew Vanessa Denny as well, didn't you? You'd guessed who the second victim was before she was identified.'

'It was a possibility. I didn't really think about it.'

'Like hell you didn't.' Brown was a very poor liar. 'How well did you know her?'

'I'd seen her with David a few times. I didn't know her very well, though.'

This was another lie, and I gave Brown a chance to reconsider. When he didn't, I rose to my feet.

'I want you to remember that this was your choice,' I said, taking a step towards him.

This was the moment when Brown lost control of his bladder.

The threat was enough. However much Brown wanted to avoid admitting to what had happened between Vanessa and himself he wanted to avoid further physical indignities far more. He caved in completely, and I could tell he wasn't holding anything back. His confession sickened me, not so much because of Vanessa's rape itself as because of what had resulted from it. Two young girls had died as a direct result of a kink in Brown's libido. Although he repeatedly insisted he hadn't realized it was anything more than an accident, all Brown was really saying was that he'd deliberately closed his eyes to the facts. The accident had been the perfect answer to all his problems, and he'd welcomed the official version with open arms. The last thing Brown had wanted was to rock the boat either by volunteering information to the police or by asking Elkhart any awkward questions. He'd carried on playing the squire and tried to pretend nothing untoward had happened.

Once I was satisfied I had it all I allowed Brown a brief respite. It was easy to see how Elkhart's warped logic would have told him Vanessa had to die. He'd gone to considerable trouble to avoid the headlines since he'd been in England, and any accusation of rape by Vanessa would have hurt him as much as it would Brown. Elkhart was accustomed to ordering accidental deaths and this must have struck him as the perfect solution. I could even guess why Mandy Collison had had to die with Vanessa. Mandy had been her friend, the only link leading back to Oxford.

I knew exactly what Mrs Robinson would have suggested if she'd been there. She'd have wanted me to go to the police. With what I had and the statement I could persuade Brown to sign I had more than enough to persuade them to re-open their investigations. However, unlike Mrs Robinson, I didn't consider this to be the point of what we were trying to do. Despite everything Brown had had to say to me, there still wasn't a single thing we could hang on to Elkhart personally. I wasn't prepared to risk seeing him walk away scot-free, and I didn't think Denny would be either.

There was also the problem of Laura to be sorted out, and she was the reason I persuaded Brown to make a phone call. Before he picked up the receiver I'd carefully coached him in what I wanted him to say.

'David?' he said. 'It's Alistair here. I thought I'd better warn you that I've just had another visit from Philis.'

Elkhart didn't answer immediately. No doubt he was taking time to enjoy a few uncharitable thoughts about me, but when he did reply his voice was as rich and mellifluous as ever.

'I'm getting sick of hearing about that man. What'd he want this time?'

'The truth.' I'd instructed Brown to keep his tone flat and unemotional. He wasn't enough of an actor to manage anything more demanding. 'He made me tell him everything.'

'Made you?'

'That's what I said. You can come and examine the bruises if you like.'

'How much did you tell him?'

139

Elkhart didn't intend to waste any time on sympathy. His interests were purely selfish.

'I told him everything I know. Philis didn't leave me with much alternative. I explained how we met in Morocco, why you're renting a house from me, what I did to Vanessa Denny. I explained it all to him.'

'I see.'

There was a brief silence which must have lasted all of five seconds. This was how long it took Elkhart to agree with me and decide that nothing Brown knew could directly implicate him in murder.

'We're finished, David,' Brown continued, responding to my nudge in the ribs. 'Philis is going to the police with what he knows. He's going to persuade them to re-open their enquiries.'

'He told you that?'

The surprise was back in Elkhart's voice.

'He did. Philis says he has enough now to convince the police that it was murder.'

'Was he going straight to the police when he left you?'

'Oh, no.' This was the crucial part and, to my surprise, Brown was handling it quite well. 'There was something to do with Laura Cunningham he has to sort out first. To be perfectly honest, I didn't quite understand what he was talking about. Is Laura staying with you?'

'Yeah, she's still here.'

'That explains it, then. Philis seemed convinced you were holding her against her will. He said this was the only thing he had left to sort out before he went to the police.'

Although their conversation continued for another five minutes or so, this marked the end of the part I'd stage-managed. On the whole, I was quite pleased with Brown's efforts. He'd delivered my message well. The bit about going to the police with my suspicions was no more than window-dressing. All Elkhart really needed to know was that I was still working on my own and that I intended to keep after him. I hoped I could leave the rest to Elkhart.

'Well?' Brown enquired nervously after he'd replaced the receiver.

'You did well,' I told him, offering a verbal pat on the head.

I knew perfectly well that this wasn't the question Brown had been asking.

'What happens to me now?' he persisted.

'Why ask me?' I said with a shrug. 'I'm no soothsayer.'

It wouldn't have been fair to have left Brown without anything at all to worry about.

CHAPTER XV

The telegram was waiting for me when I arrived back at the hotel. I read it through once at reception, then took it up to my room and read it through again. The message itself was brief, and Pawson had seen no need to put it into cipher form. It simply said 'TUOHY ARRIVED HEATHROW 09.30 YESTERDAY', and wouldn't have meant a thing to anybody who didn't know who Mr Tuohy was. I did, and I'd have to adjust my plans accordingly. The stakes hadn't changed at all, but the quality of the opposition had just undergone a dramatic improvement.

A bald statement that Tuohy was a killer would have been open to misinterpretation. There were no similarities at all between him and the kind of man who split his wife's head open with an axe because his dinner was ten minutes late. Tuohy would never act on impulse, and he'd only give his wife the chop if somebody paid him to do it. The same went for his grandmother, kids, neighbours, and all the other people in his life. Tuohy wouldn't dream of harming a hair on their heads unless somebody waved a wad of the green stuff under his nose. And it would have to be a large wad, because men like Tuohy certainly didn't sell themselves cheap.

As in any other field of human endeavour, killing had its own well-defined hierarchy. The cream at the top, the elite, were the assassins. There were never more than two or three of them at any given time, plus the occasional pretender, because there was no need for any more. These were the men who might go more than ten years between hits, and when they did work their targets had the stature of a Trujillo, a Hammarskjold or a Kennedy. None of them bore any relation at all to the man Frederick Forsyth had portrayed as his Jackal. De Gaulle would have been dead if the OAS had ever had the imagination to approach the true killer elite.

Next in rank came the enforcers, the men like Anastasia, who did the dirty work for organized crime. They were the best argument for omerta that there was. However, the category which most interested Pawson and his counterparts in other security agencies were the freelances, the have-gun-will-travel types. SR(2) had at least a dozen of them on file that I knew about and, whenever possible, the department tried to keep some sort of trace on them. In the past Pawson had even recruited one or two of the freelances to perform specific jobs for him, and this was precisely why he tried to keep such a close eye on them. If he'd thought of using them it was a pound to a penny that the heads of other departments would have had similar thoughts.

Tuohy wasn't important enough, or good enough, to figure on Pawson's list. He was one of the also-rans, deadly enough in his own way but more of a mechanic than a craftsman. In any case, Pawson didn't normally bother to keep me informed of arrivals to and departures from the UK by contract killers. He'd had a very special reason for telling me about Tuohy. According to the FBI report we'd both read at least two of the deaths connected to the Messengers in the States had been put out to contract. They'd been too important or too delicate to be handled by the home-grown Messenger muscle. In both instances the FBI suspected it was Tuohy who had been used, a supposition that was given

142

added weight by the fact that both Tuohy and Elkhart had attended the same college at the same time. It was perfectly feasible that Tuohy's arrival was unconnected, but I preferred to assume it wasn't. Whatever else he might be, he was a professional of a sort and I couldn't afford to treat him lightly.

It was hardly a surprise to discover that Laura was to be the chosen agent of my destruction. I'd just finished a call to London to confirm that a photo of and breakdown on Tuohy were on their way, and was washing, when the telephone beside the bed rang. I wiped the soap out of my eyes and went across the room to answer it.

'It's Laura,' Laura said.

I practised an unforgiving silence. Other ears would be listening apart from Laura's.

'I'm at the cottage,' she persevered. 'I have to see you, Philis. It's urgent.'

'You're too late,' I told her. 'I came looking for you last night. You said everything you had to say then.'

'Oh, Philis.' The words came out like a wail. 'For goodness' sake, you weren't taken in by that, were you? Elkhart forced me to behave the way I did. He didn't give me any choice.'

'Sure,' I said before I hung up. 'I saw the weapon he was using to intimidate you.'

Of course, I'd no intention of leaving matters there. My opinions hadn't changed since the previous night, I was simply playing the odds. If, by some remote chance, Laura really was a free agent, she'd have to make this clear to me. It was only about twenty minutes down the road. If, on the other hand, Laura's phone call had signified the first of Elkhart's counter-measures, she'd definitely be phoning again. The second call came shortly after four.

'It's Laura again, Philis. Please, please listen to me.'

She was crying. At the back of my mind I wondered whether the tears were assumed or whether somebody had

143

been doing something to make her cry.

'I'm listening,' I said, making it sound like a grudging concession.

'Listen, Philis. No matter how bad it looked and sounded, last night wasn't at all what it seemed. Elkhart threatened to kill me unless I did exactly as he said.'

I kept silent. Despite her obvious distress, I wasn't doing anything to encourage her.

'Please, Philis, won't you come out to the cottage and give me a chance to explain properly?'

'Why don't you come to the hotel? You know the way.'

'I would have done, but I don't think I'm in a fit state to drive. Besides, I'm not in the mood to face other people at the moment.'

It was quite a good answer, well backed up by bucketfuls of tears. I decided to test Laura to see how fully she'd been briefed.

'There's one thing that doesn't make sense to me,' I told her. 'Last night you claim Elkhart was threatening to kill you in order to force you to do things against your will. Today you're as free as a bird. How exactly do you account for his sudden change of heart?'

'That's part of what I want to explain to you, Philis.' Laura had the answer off pat, even if it wasn't nearly as convincing as her previous effort. 'You will come, won't you?'

'OK.' If our conversation had been for real, wild horses wouldn't have dragged me near the cottage, but I was fed up with messing around. 'I'll pop over late, but don't harbour any mistaken ideas. I shan't be staying long.'

'What time can I expect you?'

Laura was crying again.

'It will probably be about nine,' I told her. 'I have a couple of other calls to make first.'

This was the sentence I chose to hang up on. When I re-ran it through my mind I found the conversation just as unsatisfactory in retrospect as it had been at the time. There hadn't even been any real attempt to convince me it was genuine, a feature which suggested unwonted confidence in the enemy camp. I hoped I'd be able to redress the balance by arriving at the rendezvous a few hours early.

This should have been the time to call in the police, to wave my identity card under senior officers' noses and demand their co-operation. Unfortunately, it would have taken far too long, and I doubted whether the local constabulary had been trained to cope with the likes of Tuohy. All the same, I'd no intention of walking into a trap without giving myself some kind of edge, however minimal. Two attempts to contact Mrs Robinson at the Golden Lion were unsuccessful, but I did leave her a message for when she'd finished detecting for the day. I also made one or two other arrangements which, hopefully, would make me considerably less vulnerable than Elkhart and company would be anticipating. About the only thing I didn't do was file a full report for Pawson. This would have smacked too much of a Last Will and Testament.

For the last mile I walked, working my way across the fields so that I came on the cottage from behind. This put me above Laura's home, which was perched half-way up a hill, and I spent ten minutes with the binoculars, lying in the snow underneath a hedge. What I saw didn't prove much one way or another. The lights were on downstairs; I caught occasional glimpses of Laura's silhouette as she walked in front of the windows; and there were no signs of anybody else. In other words, it was all pretty much as I'd expected.

In the absence of any hard facts upon which to base my calculations, there was necessarily a large element of guesswork in my plans. I had to make assumptions, and the pivotal one placed a gentleman called Tuohy inside the cottage, waiting for me to make my move. It was also a safe bet that his plans didn't include simply gunning me down. If this had been his intention, there were a lot of better places to do it where there would have been no need for such an elaborate

145

set-up. Laura and I were almost certainly scheduled for another of Elkhart's little accidents. There was one final assumption I could make with a fair degree of confidence. Tuohy was a professional, and he would have taken the nine o'clock I'd mentioned with a pinch of salt. No matter what time I arrived at the cottage the American gunman would be ready for me.

By now I was getting wet lying in the snow and I'd run out of assumptions. However, when I left the shelter of the hedge, I didn't head directly for the cottage itself. I preferred to backtrack a little and work my way along the hedgerows in the general direction of the small stand of trees which adjoined Laura's property. I'd no way of knowing whether Tuohy was working mob-handed or not, but I intended to behave as though he was. In Tuohy's position I'd have had at least one man outside the cottage, and the copse would have been far and away the best place to position him.

Twenty-five yards from my destination I ran out of hedges. I didn't fancy crawling on my stomach through the frozen beet, and nothing on earth would have persuaded me down into the ditch. The sound of fracturing ice would instantly have alerted anybody in the trees, the same way my screams would have done once the freezing water got to work on my lower extremities. The only alternative was to be patient and wait. It was almost ten minutes before I received my reward in the shape of a solitary car starting the climb up the road in front of the cottage. I waited until the vehicle was fairly close, its headlights shining on the trees ahead of me, before I started to run. Although it was impossible to be quiet, the noise of the labouring engine was guaranteed to drown any other sounds.

As soon as I reached the first of the trees I dropped to the ground again, using some brambles for camouflage. Although it wasn't much of a copse there were far too many of the stunted trees for me to have any hope of spotting anybody who didn't want to be spotted. Fortunately, man's hunting instincts had been blunted millennia ago, and Carl had never

146

bothered to learn how to keep still. The slight movement of his feet gave me a rough fix within a minute or so, and a smothered cough a few minutes later enabled me to pinpoint him. Three cars and twenty minutes later I could actually see where Carl was wedged in between two trees. It was interesting to note that he spent almost as much time watching the fields as he did the road. Tuohy had evidently coached him well.

I'd been kneading the snowball for so long it was virtually a lump of ice. When I threw it I went for height as much as distance, and it made a lot of noise coming down through the branches. Carl was only human, so both his face and shotgun were pointing in the opposite direction when I stepped up behind him and began to break his neck. Much as he objected, there was nothing he could do to stop me, and even the shotgun was nothing more than an encumbrance. As I steadily increased the pressure Carl could actually hear his neck beginning to go. We'd reached the critical point, the stage where a twist and a pull were all that stood between Carl and death, when I stopped.

'I'd try to stand very still,' I advised him, whispering into his ear. 'It would be a shame to kill you when I didn't mean to.'

This was all I had to say to turn him into a statue. He knew enough about human anatomy to realize he shouldn't be able to look down between his shoulderblades at his heels.

'In a minute,' I said, 'I am going to ease the pressure a little, and when I do you're going to start talking very quietly. I want to hear everything you know about Mr Tuohy.'

Although he was far too frightened to put all his thoughts in the correct order, Carl did his best to be co-operative. While he didn't manage to come up with anything particularly startling, he gave me enough for me to be able to base the next step on fact instead of assumption. However, there was one glaring omission in what Carl had to say.

'What about Steven?' I whispered. 'Where exactly does your friend fit in?'

'Steve?' Despite his fear and the awkward position he was being held in, the surprise still showed through. 'As far as I know he's back at the house with the Reverend David.'

'You're sure about that, are you?'

I gingered him up a little by taking his neck a little closer to fracture point but it didn't change his story. More important, I was inclined to believe him. It seemed that Tuohy was all I had left to deal with.

Carl stayed up in the copse, secured to the same two trees he'd been hiding behind, and his shotgun went with me. Despite what he'd told me, and my acceptance of it, I carefully checked all the other potential places of concealment outside the cottage. When my life was at stake I never took anything on trust. Besides, I had an indefinable sense of something wrong. After I'd failed to find anything which confirmed this I had to hope I'd simply become too keyed-up. Even so, I still felt my progress to date had been suspiciously easy.

The nagging doubt was still at the back of my mind when I reached the phone-box a hundred yards from the cottage. Tuohy would have worked on contingency plans for most of the ways I might try to get to Laura, but I hoped I was about to teach him something new. I'd be matching my tactics to the terrain, just like I'd been taught back at the SR(2) training school.

'It's Philis,' I said when Laura answered the phone.

'Philis?' The strain and tension were immediately apparent in her voice. 'What do you want? You are still coming to see me, aren't you?'

'That all depends,' I told her. 'First of all I want to speak to Mr Tuohy.'

'What on earth are you talking about, Philis? I'm at the cottage on my own. I don't even know anybody called Tuohy.'

Despite the few seconds she'd had to prepare the lies they were clumsy and unconvincing. Laura was crumbling fast.

148

and I was glad I hadn't delayed my arrival any longer.

'Charade time is over, love,' I explained. 'I know exactly what's been happening, and it's important I speak to Tuohy. What I have to say to him may save a lot of people from being hurt.'

Laura put her hand over the mouthpiece so she could speak to Tuohy, and I put down the receiver in the telephone box. Then I was outside and running. Timing was everything, so delicate that a second either way could totally upset the balance. As soon as the phone first rang Tuohy would have been suspicious. He'd have immediately suspected a diversion, and he'd be alert for trouble. Hopefully, though, I would have drawn a lot of his teeth. I shouldn't have known his name. I shouldn't even have known he was in the country. Self-preservation would decree that Tuohy would have to speak to me, whatever his misgivings, if only to discover how I'd learned about him. He'd run a quick check of the cottage's doors and windows first, but in a few seconds he'd have to pick up the receiver. This same few seconds was how long I had to reach the front door.

Once I was there there were a few seconds of fumbling with the key I'd taken from Carl along with the shotgun, then I was inside the small entrance hall, leaving the front door open behind me.

'Hello, hello,' I could hear Tuohy say. 'Who's this?'

It seemed I'd arrived barely in time, but barely was plenty long enough. I knew precisely where the telephone was in relation to the door I was coming through. I knew where Tuohy would be standing, well back against the wall so he wouldn't present a target at either of the windows. All I had left to do was throw open the door and point the shotgun.

What impressed me most about Tuohy wasn't his initial reaction, even though there was hardly any time-lag between the door banging open and his response. I'd met a lot of people who could have managed that. Tuohy demonstrated his a little touch of class when he aborted the idea almost the same moment it had occurred to him, halting the movement of his hand towards the automatic which lay beside the telephone. He was good enough to realize his limitations, and sane enough not to want to be blasted in half with a shotgun. I didn't have to warn him about his hands, either. He raised them above his head straight away, showing me he had no aggressive intentions.

'That was sneaky,' he said with a thin smile.

'Thanks for the compliment. Let's have your hands just a little bit closer to the ceiling. Then turn around to face the wall.'

Tuohy saved us a little more time by adopting the correct posture straight away, feet well apart and with all the weight taken on his hands. I moved up behind him, jamming the muzzle of the shotgun against the underside of his jaw while I checked him for concealed weapons. Although the metal was gouging into his flesh it was the best guarantee I could have that Tuohy wouldn't become ambitious.

While I was doing this, Laura was busy unravelling her emotions. She'd sunk down on to the sofa as though her legs wouldn't support her any longer, and she was obviously having trouble believing I really was in the cottage. Unless she'd worked out the bit with the phone-box, I could understand her problem.

'How many others are there?' I asked her.

I'd left Tuohy against the wall, but I'd moved back to stand beside Laura.

'Just one.' It sounded as though she found speaking something of an effort but it was the answer I'd wanted to hear. Despite what Carl had told me, I'd been worrying about Steven. 'He's outside the cottage somewhere. He must have seen you arrive.'

A touch of hysteria had come into Laura's voice when she realized her ordeal might not be over after all and she started to stand up. I put a hand on her shoulder to calm her down.

'Don't panic,' I told her. 'I dealt with Carl on the way in. I just wanted to be sure there wasn't anybody else.'

'No. Carl was the only one.'

When Laura spoke she sounded curiously stilted, and I thought I knew why. She wasn't simply relieved, she was embarrassed as well because she was convinced she owed me an enormous apology. Later on, when I had the time, I'd have to explain that she'd behaved in the only possible way. Dead heroines were only attractive in the pages of fiction.

'I'd like a few words alone with Mr Tuohy here,' I said. 'Can you go into the kitchen and make some coffee or something? I'll only be a few minutes.'

'All right, but . . . '

I interrupted Laura there, sensing an apology on the way.

'Save all the buts for later,' I suggested. 'Just concentrate on the coffee for now.'

Tuohy hadn't moved a muscle while we'd been talking, or while Laura was walking to the kitchen. I didn't think he was likely to unless I gave him a specific order. Tuohy was paid to kill people, not to take senseless risks.

It was difficult to know exactly how to handle Tuohy. He was what I'd come to the cottage for and now I had him I wasn't sure what to do with him. My biggest drawback was that all I really knew about him was he killed people for a living, and there weren't many physical clues to his character. 'Ordinary' was the word which suited his appearance best. Tuohy was medium height, medium build, medium everything you cared to mention. Even though I was watching him closely and knew precisely how he made his money, I couldn't spot any major flaws in his camouflage. He was very light and balanced on his feet, but I didn't think I would have recognized him for what he was unless I'd had prior warning.

'You'll be more comfortable on the sofa,' I told him. 'Keep your hands up on your head, though.'

Once again, Tuohy moved very carefully, anxious not to do anything which might alarm me. He wasn't at all afraid. He was simply biding his time, looking for a way out, and I was perfectly prepared to throw him some kind of lifeline.

'What does Elkhart mean to you?' I asked.

Tuohy shrugged, his face expressionless. He wasn't certain what I was after.

'He's a client,' he said.

'So I gathered.' Tuohy obviously didn't intend to give anything away. 'I also happen to know that the two of you were at college together, and that Elkhart has employed your services before. I was wondering if there was some kind of special relationship.'

On this occasion Tuohy was slower to answer, and I hoped it was because I'd worried him. I knew a lot more about his private life than I should have done. I'd also given him some indication of what I was after.

'I suppose you could say I'm like a hooker,' he said carefully. 'With most of the customers it's a once-in-a-lifetime deal. With a very few of them, like Elkhart, it's different. Do a good job and there's likely to be plenty of repeat business.'

'So you don't owe Elkhart anything?'

'That isn't quite true. When I accept a contract, I take half the fee in advance.'

He wasn't raising any serious objection to the delicate negotiations I'd initiated. He was making sure I was aware of the exact situation.

'We may be able to do business,' I told him. 'If it came to a choice between doing a long spell in prison or blowing the whistle on Elkhart, which way would you go?'

'You're not offering me much choice, are you?'

Although Tuohy was deliberately being non-committal, we both knew what his reply would have to be.

'What do you expect?' I asked. 'Besides, I'd have said I was being generous. It's a question of priorities. Elkhart is the man I'm after, and all I have is you. Give me something which will help to nail Elkhart down and I'll be quite happy to toss you back into the sea.'

'And how am I supposed to do that? Deliver Elkhart, I mean.'

'You should know the answer better than I do. You've

worked for Elkhart before. You must have plenty I can use.'

Whether Tuohy did or not was something I'd never know. When the kitchen door opened behind me I didn't even bother to turn my head. I assumed it must be Laura returning with the coffee. Once Steven had the cold metal of the second shotgun pressed against the back of my neck I couldn't have turned my head even if I'd wanted to. I hadn't had anything to teach Tuohy after all. He really had planned for every contingency.

'It never pays to underestimate people, Philis,' Tuohy said softly.

'Sure,' I answered. 'That should make a great obituary.'

In a way I had to admire him. Neither Carl nor Laura had been lying when they'd told me Steven wasn't anywhere around. They'd been telling me the truth as they'd known it, because Tuohy hadn't wanted to run any risks of them giving his plans away. He'd deliberately put himself at risk, using himself as bait, because he'd realized this was the only way he could take me without having to damage me. To achieve this Tuohy must have kept Steven away from the immediate vicinity of the cottage, somewhere he could observe without being at any risk of being discovered himself. What annoyed me most was that I hadn't simply walked into his trap, I'd rushed into it, convinced that I was the one doing the out-smarting. If I ever lived long enough to write them, this was yet another episode I'd be glossing over in my memoirs.

CHAPTER XVI

I knew I should have killed Tuohy while I'd had the chance. Without him, Carl and Steven would look very ordinary indeed. With him they constituted a formidable team which was shortly going to kill Laura and myself. Laura probably saw some cause for optimism in the fact that neither of us was tied, but I was more experienced in the ways of the world.

Accident victims begin to lose a lot of their credibility when the police discover rope-burns on wrists and ankles.

To date there had been no indication of what kind of accident Tuohy had planned for us. Carl and Steven were off somewhere, presumably making preparations for our disposal, and I knew I'd have to try to do something before their return. So far I hadn't decided what. Laura and I were sitting silently in the armchairs, acting under instructions, while Tuohy himself had taken the chair by the telephone. It might be less comfortable than our seats, but he had a gun to compensate, and there was a damn great sofa as a barricade between him and me. I could think of scores of ways of getting myself killed, and only one of reaching Tuohy. It was the kind of long-shot which was strictly a last resort. All the same, it did offer me some encouragement. A top gun wouldn't have left me with even a longshot.

'It's not too late to change your mind,' I said. 'I shan't think any the worse of you if you do.'

'You're wasting your breath, Philis,' he responded curtly. 'You know how the system works as well as I do. I don't have nearly enough to retire on yet.'

This took me one step closer to my last resort. It had been the wrong approach, and I knew it. A contract killer like Tuohy relied on word of mouth for new clients, and he was only worth as much as his last kill. Word of mouth could also ruin him, because once a pro accepted a target no allowances were made for failure. Somebody like Tuohy would need to have a really compelling motive to back out on a contract, and I wasn't at all sure I could provide him with one. Nevertheless, this was another avenue I had to explore.

'Tell me something,' I said. 'Do you have any idea who I am?'

'You're supposed to be some kind of private investigator, aren't you?'

'That's the way I described myself when I first came into the area, but I'm a notorious liar. Do you mind if I get out my wallet?'

154

'Go ahead.'

There was only the slightest of hesitations before he agreed. I'd already been searched for weapons, and Tuohy knew he could do me irreparable harm long before I could be a threat to him. The very fact that I still had a wallet and the rest of my personal effects was further proof of the scheduled accident. I'd be expected to have things in my pockets when I died.

My identity card, the genuine one, was in a special concealed compartment at the back of my wallet. I was only supposed to flash it around in an emergency, and I considered this a pretty fair description of my current predicament.

'Shall I bring it over to you?'

'Don't bother.' Tuohy was matching my smile with one of his own. 'Just throw it on the sofa.'

I allowed him a few seconds to examine what I'd given him. I very much doubted whether SR(2) would mean anything to him, but I could see Tuohy had the general idea. There was a new appraising look in his eyes when he raised his head again.

'Is it a government department?'

'It is, and it has a lot of international connections. That's how I knew you were in the country.'

'I see.'

Tuohy had suddenly discovered he had a lot of rethinking to do. Although he wasn't sharing his thoughts with me, there was no need. I'd anticipated his dilemma when I'd decided to reveal my identity to him. Unless he was crazy, which I didn't think he was, Tuohy would never have accepted the contract if he'd been in possession of all the facts. There was a definite limit to what he'd consider an acceptable risk.

'Does Elkhart know who you are?' he asked.

'What do you think?'

He thought precisely what I'd intended him to, because my tone of voice had been guaranteed to give him the wrong

155

impression. I wasn't entirely sure why I'd bothered. The wedge I'd driven between him and Elkhart would make very little difference to what happened to me. Tuohy would be more annoyed by his own negligence than by Elkhart's supposed duplicity. I certainly hadn't given him enough to persuade him to break his contract. He was too far committed for that.

'You're in a bit of a spot, aren't you?' I said encouragingly. 'Your name is pencilled in as the author of the crime even before it's been committed.'

'You've got it wrong, Philis.' Tuohy's composure was a measure of how much success I was having. 'There's not going to be any crime. You're going to have a little accident.'

Although Laura hadn't been an active participant in the conversation she'd been paying close attention to what we'd said. When Tuohy mentioned an accident she looked across at me, seeking some form of reassurance. Even if I'd had any to offer, I wouldn't have spared her any of my attention. It was Tuohy I had to deal with.

'Aren't you being rather naïve?' The contempt in my voice was carefully calculated. 'It isn't the police you have to worry about. The people I work for don't have any more faith in accidents than they do in fairy tales. They've arranged too many themselves. If anything happens to me, they're going to come looking for you.'

'Why? They don't know I'm involved in anything.'

Tuohy sounded sceptical.

'Like I said, we're not the police. Rule number one where I live is that you never, ever turn the other cheek, not unless you want your head knocked off. We don't allow anybody to take liberties with us. Kill me, and there isn't anywhere on earth you'll be safe.'

It was almost a full minute before Tuohy smiled, shaking his head as he did so. I'd come close, but in my position close was nowhere.

'No,' he said. 'Sorry, but I don't think it's gonna work like that. Maybe they'll put me somewhere on your department's shit list, but I sure won't be worth an all-out manhunt. As long as I keep away from any of your people from now on, they're not going to put out a contract on me. It's not worth it.'

I found it very hard to dispute Tuohy's logic, which was something of a shame. Now I'd have to try to kill him.

The trick was to think positive. Tuohy might have the gun, but I had to be the one with all the confidence because I was moving into an area where logic had no place. Since I'd run out of alternatives, there was no point in considering what might go wrong. Unless I was totally and irrevocably committed when I tried for Tuohy there wasn't any sense in making the effort. I might as well sit back and let him kill me.

Besides, I had advantages Tuohy knew nothing about. To begin with there was the sofa, a big, solid piece of furniture which helped to make him feel secure. While that was between us there was no way I could make a straight run at him. I'd have to stop to climb over the damn thing, and while I was doing that Tuohy would have time to empty his automatic and reload. At least, this was what Tuohy thought. I knew something he didn't, something I'd discovered on my second visit to the cottage. The sofa stood on a carpet, and the carpet was resting on a highly-polished parquet floor. If Laura could slide it around without too much effort so could I.

Then there was Tuohy's gun. It was a nice enough gun, as deadly a weapon as you could hope to find anywhere, but it was also heavy. Anybody who held it for any length of time would soon begin to feel as though his arm was about to drop off. Tuohy was well aware of this. He knew the weight would make his hand tremble, and this would spoil his marksmanship. Consequently, he'd done the sensible thing. He'd moved back a safe distance, he'd made sure there was a large piece of furniture between us, and he'd put down the automatic. It was only a few inches away from his hand, on the table beside the telephone. However fast I moved he

157

could pick it up and be using it before I was half-way across the room towards him. He'd no way of knowing I didn't want to go all the way, and this was no coy virgin talk. All I wanted to do was reach the sofa.

When the time came for me to make my move it would all boil down to a question of time – I had to reach the sofa before Tuohy shot me. On this basis I had a couple of other factors going for me. Neither of them was worth more than a few hundredths of a second to me, but tiny fractions of a second were going to make all the difference between life and death. Although I already knew Tuohy's reflexes were sharp, quite possibly as sharp as my own, his own brain thinking was going to slow him down. Shooting me would be a last resort. His whole strategy had been geared towards an apparent accident, a killing which would reveal no hint of foul play. Tuohy would try to shoot me to protect himself, but he'd be slow off the mark. Or, to be more accurate, he wouldn't be quite as fast as usual.

'Don't you have anything else to say?'

Tuohy was gently mocking me.

'Not that I can think of.'

'You haven't tried to buy me off yet. You could always offer me more than Elkhart is paying.'

'On my salary? You must be joking.'

I was finding it increasingly difficult not to keep glancing at the clock. It would be impossible for Tuohy to guess what I was waiting for, but too great a display of interest would inevitably put him on his guard.

'How about you?' Tuohy was addressing himself to Laura now. 'Are you going to try to talk yourself out of an early grave?'

'I wouldn't know where to begin.' It was a brave effort, but Laura didn't have quite the control she would have liked. The odd quavering was clearly discernible. 'I don't have anything to offer which would interest you.'

'Come off it,' Tuohy objected. 'You're a good-looking woman, I'm only human.'

158

He was simply amusing himself, whiling away the time until Carl and Steven came back. I couldn't afford the luxury of any such distraction. The best I could do was blot out his and Laura's voices and commence another mental rehearsal of what I intended to do. The waiting had been bad enough before when I was afraid the others might return before I was ready. Now nine o'clock had come and gone, and nothing had happened. Out of the corner of my eye I could see that the clock hands had crawled to two minutes past the hour.

'. . . Philis?'

I hadn't been listening, and I didn't have the remotest idea what Tuohy had asked me, but it didn't matter. The telephone started to ring almost as he finished speaking, and this was what I'd been waiting for, the point where pre-programming took over. As I came up out of my chair I was aware of Tuohy's inadvertent glance to his right, towards the telephone. These were the last few hundredths of a second I'd been gambling on, but I'd have gone just the same even if Tuohy had proved to be inhuman and refused to bat an eyelid. There was no other option open to me.

I came out of the chair low and hard, driving and pushing with my legs as I hurled myself at the bottom of the sofa, staking my life on a waxed floor. For an instant after impact it didn't seem as though the sofa was going to move. Then it began to slide, just as I'd known it should, and I was putting every last ounce of strength and desperation into my drive because by now Tuohy would have the gun in his hand.

It was a very close-run thing and a lot of things seemed to happen at once. Laura screamed, I smashed the sofa into Tuohy and his gun went off. Fortunately all he succeeded in hitting was the sofa, and he didn't do it nearly as much damage as the sofa did to him. Even though the chair and telephone table had absorbed some of the shock, most of the air had been forcibly driven out of his lungs, and he found himself the middle part of a sandwich between the wall and the sofa.

Although I'd hurt him, hurting wasn't enough, not when he still had a gun. Now I was driving upwards in a continuation of my original movement, the fingers of my left hand clamping on to his wrist just before he fired for a second time. The bullet went close, but it missed, whining harmlessly past me, and after this it was no contest.

Tuohy was a mechanic, an expert on guns and the other paraphernalia of death. He was a specialist, not an all-rounder like me, and if his chosen weapon failed him he didn't have a great deal to fall back on. I hadn't stopped at his wrist. I'd continued my upward surge, my right forearm held as rigid as an iron bar in front of me, and it caught Tuohy under the chin, smashing his head back against the wall. I wedged it there for a few seconds, ignoring what Tuohy was doing with his spare hand while I worked away at the one holding the gun. Once he'd decided it would be less painful to drop the weapon I should have had a choice, but I'd made my mind up in advance. Although Tuohy's testimony would have knocked the final few nails into Elkhart's coffin, his potential nuisance value if I had to deal with Carl and Steven more than outweighed his usefulness. I'd have to nail Elkhart on Laura's evidence alone.

When I abruptly released Tuohy and stepped back he was taken completely by surprise. It probably didn't even occur to him that I was merely allowing myself room to move. He stood there, trapped by the sofa, and he completely bought my feint, turning into the blow which counted. I did hit him a second time, but I knew deep down that this hadn't been necessary.

Now it was over I didn't turn around immediately, I knew I was being irrational but I was worried about what Laura might think of me. OK, I'd just saved her life and she already knew enough about the department to realize I was no Boy Scout but what she'd witnessed had been far from pretty. Perhaps I felt the odd pang of guilt because I knew I hadn't killed Tuohy in the heat of battle. I'd done it as a matter of policy, with plenty of malice and forethought thrown in, and

I wasn't quite sure how this would affect my standing in her eyes.

This was a question which became totally immaterial when I did turn around and realized where the stray bullet had gone. Laura had no longer been able to see when I finished Tuohy, but I still thought I could detect reproach in the sightless eyes.

Head wounds weren't necessarily fatal, no matter how messy they looked. There were even occasions when the blood was a good sign. Laura certainly looked dead, but this wasn't something I could take for granted, and checking her took priority over everything else. It only took a few seconds, but this proved to be a few seconds too long.

It was a mistake I should never have made. I'd known Carl and Steven were due back at any moment. This was why I'd been so worried that they might turn up before the pre-arranged phone call from Mrs Robinson had provided me with the cue I'd been waiting for. My error had been in the assumption that they'd be returning by car and I'd have plenty of warning of their arrival. It should have occurred to me that one of the most essential preparations they'd be making was to shift some of the spare vehicles away from the vicinity of the cottage. It was a mistake I became aware of while I was still bending over Laura.

'Well, well, well,' Carl said from behind me, speaking from the door which led into the entrance hall. 'You have been busy while we were away.'

I didn't even have Tuohy's Walther. Concern for Laura had taken precedence over scrabbling behind the sofa to retrieve the weapon. Even so, I might have been tempted to try something if I hadn't heard Steven coming through the kitchen. The two of them hadn't walked in cold, expecting to find Tuohy in control. Everything about them, right down to the way their shotguns were cocked, suggested that they'd been anticipating trouble. They might even have been outside the cottage when the shots had been fired. This would have given them plenty of warning of what to expect.

Once he was in the room, Steven seemed to appreciate the changes which had taken place while he'd been absent. He looked around him, then gave a long, low whistle.

'Is Tuohy dead?' he asked Carl.

'I don't know. Is he?'

The question was addressed to me and I shrugged.

'He should be,' I told him.

'The poor old sod.' Steven's laugh belied his words. 'That's going to save David a dollar or two.'

'It's going to mean more work for us,' Carl pointed out. 'We'll have to do the job ourselves.'

The prospect didn't appear to upset him noticeably. I tried to deflate him a little. Although it wasn't a subject I'd normally have chosen for discussion, I had a vested interest in hurrying things along.

'You're going to need a change of plan,' I said. 'Accidents don't seem quite so convincing when one of the victims has a bullet-hole in her.'

'That's a very good point.' Carl still sounded cheerful enough. 'I don't suppose you'd like to explain what's been happening here.'

'You suppose right.'

For a second or two Carl and I tried to outstare each other. It was left to Steven to break the awkward silence.

'Philis is right, you know,' he told Carl. 'An accident is out of the question. Even if we fixed it so she didn't surface we'd never be able to do anything about the blood all over the place.'

'Now we have Tuohy's body we don't need an accident any more.' Although Carl wasn't one of the most likeable young men I'd ever met, he was no fool. 'We'll leave the woman here, along with Tuohy's gun. It should have his prints all over it.'

'What about the other two? Do we dump them like we planned?'

'That's it, Steve.' Every word Carl spoke was aimed at me

The various indignities he'd suffered at my hands obviously rankled. 'We'll still have our burial at sea. It might even be more effective than the way we originally planned it. The police won't be able to make head or tail of it, and there won't be anything leading back to us.'

'What's that about the sea?'

I was trying to look nervous and cowed, and I wasn't finding this too difficult.

'Haven't you heard?' Carl was clearly delighted by my question. 'We're taking you for a little cruise.'

'Perhaps his girl-friend didn't take him into her confidence about her boat,' Steven put in. 'After all, she didn't tell him about David, did she?'

Both of them had a big laugh out of this, but I didn't join in. I was becoming increasingly impatient. If they intended to kill me, why the hell didn't they forget the chatter and get on with it?

CHAPTER XVII

I belonged to the generation which had helped to lose the British Empire. The tradition of Drake and Nelson had died away in the fusty pages of history books. As messing about in boats had never played any part in my upbringing, all the sea did for me was make me feel vaguely nauseous. For the moment, though, I had too many other things to worry about for my stomach to have a high priority. We were buffeting through the choppy waters of the Ouse estuary, and time was running out. So far, Carl and Steven had given me no opportunity to get anywhere near them and I wasn't likely to while I was squatting on the cabin floor with my left wrist handcuffed to a metal table leg. As the table leg was screwed firmly to the floor I was going to experience great difficulty moving anywhere.

163

'What am I supposed to be doing out here?' I asked. 'That's the first thing the police are going to wonder, and they're not likely to believe I'm pioneering mid-winter North Sea cruises.'

'It doesn't really matter what they think.' Steven was at the wheel, so Carl was the one pointing the automatic shotgun at me from the far end of the lounge. 'The more the police have to puzzle them, the less likely they are to come up with the right answer.'

'That doesn't sound like Tuohy's planning. From what I've heard he was supposed to be an expert.'

At the moment Tuohy's body was lying on the carpet between us. It wouldn't be long before rigor mortis started to set in.

'His idea won't work any more.' Carl seemed quite happy to talk. 'He'd intended to arrange an explosion at the boat's mooring. Mrs Cunningham would have been showing you over her boat when the accident happened. She'd have been showing you how smoothly the engine ran, without remembering to run the blowers or check the bilge.'

'And that would cause an explosion?'

I really didn't know anything about boats, even luxury craft like Laura's.

'That's what I asked Tuohy when he was explaining it to me.' Carl actually favoured me with a smile. 'Apparently gas fumes can build up in the bilge. It only needs a spark to detonate them.'

Carl said gas, but I assumed he meant petrol.

'And you don't know how to set it up?'

'Steve and I aren't mechanics. All the same, we've managed to come up with a pretty good alternative. I'd say it was even something of an improvement.'

It took Carl almost a quarter of an hour to explain what he had in store for me. Although I kept my opinion to myself, I didn't think it was an improvement at all. On the contrary, the plan was every bit as sloppy and untidy as I might have expected from a couple of cowboys. Unfortunately, it also

164

sounded as though it might work, and dead was dead, no matter how sloppily or untidily death was caused.

According to Carl's masterplan I was still scheduled to be blown sky-high but certain changes had become necessary. As Carl had already said, Tuohy had kept the actual mechanics of his plan to himself. All Carl and Steven had inherited from him was a time-pencil detonator and the germ of an idea. Their alternative, clumsy as it was, did display a certain ingenuity.

The Wash was about two hundred square miles of tidal estuary, with rivers like the Ouse, Nene and Welland emptying into it. At low tide, as it was now, the river water reached the sea through winding channels cut into the exposed banks of sand and mud. The 'Laura' was going to be run aground on one of the sandbanks in the middle of the Wash and this was where Carl and Steven intended to rig the whole boat into a kind of nautical time-bomb. Before they left in the runabout which was being towed behind the 'Laura' they'd turn on the main gas cylinders in the galley, crush the glass ampoule of the time-pencil and say goodbye to me. If everything worked according to plan, au revoir would be inappropriate.

However, this wasn't enough for them. It was a two-hour time-pencil, allowing for a sufficient build-up of gas to blast me halfway to the moon. On the other hand, they didn't know enough about what they were doing to be absolutely certain the detonator would ignite the gas and this was why they had a fail-safe. If their calculations were wrong, the last thing they wanted was for the rising tide to lift the 'Laura' clear of the sandbank and drift it gently back into harbour with a manacled Philis still aboard.

Yet again Carl and Steven's thoughts had a kind of crazy logic to them. Knock a few large holes in the bottom of the boat and, even if the explosion didn't happen, the boat would sink as soon as there was sufficient water under the keel. Although I didn't say so to Carl, it all seemed like a hell of a waste of time and effort because I should never have left Laura's cottage alive. Carl and Steven didn't seem to realize that Tuohy had only been prepared to go to so much trouble because he was trying to stage an accident. Perhaps they thought all their messing about was the professional way. Or perhaps they got a kick out of freezing their balls off in the middle of the Wash. Whatever their reason, I was grateful to them. They were offering me a chance where one should never have been allowed.

After Carl had finished I had nothing to do except wait for the bump when we went aground. Although Steven shouted down a warning before we hit, Tuohy was in no state to brace himself and his body ended up under the table with me. I wasn't sure whether the reproach in his eyes was for me or for the clowns who had taken over from him.

I didn't completely give up on the shotgun, but I did begin to contemplate alternative strategies for when I was alone on the *Laura*. None of them had any great appeal, or held out any great prospect of success, but they were all that was left to me. I certainly had no intention of dying easily.

Steven must have experienced greater difficulty in knocking a hole in the bottom of the boat than he'd anticipated. We'd been aground for almost twenty minutes before he appeared, axe in one hand, the second shotgun in the other. It had been twenty minutes when Carl had shown no indication of coming closer to me, and I'd failed abysmally in my efforts to dream up some means of luring him within range.

'We're ready to go,' Steven announced.

'You've done a proper job, have you?'

'Go and take a look for yourself. This boat should go down like a stone once she has some water under her. Let's hope it's a wasted precaution.'

It only took Carl a couple of minutes to check.

'Satisfied?'

Steven sounded disgruntled. He hadn't thought it necessary for Carl to inspect his work.

'You done good, boy,' Carl said with a smile, attempting to parody a Southern accent. 'You'd better go and see what you can do with the outboard. I'll rig the galley once you're ready.'

'What about Philis?' Steven still wasn't placated. 'Are we just going to leave him here?'

'I don't see why not. He doesn't have anywhere to go.'

'So you keep on telling me,' Steven said stubbornly. 'I still think it would make more sense to shoot him before we leave. We're not trying to fake an accident any longer, so it won't make any difference.'

'It would, Steve, it would. Shooting would be far too quick for Philis. I want him to have time to think about what's going to happen to him.'

Although Steven clearly wasn't happy, Carl was the dominant one of the pair, and there were no more objections. Steven went to prepare the dinghy, leaving me with Carl again.

'Well,' he prompted after a moment or two. 'Don't you have any last words to say?'

I shrugged my shoulders.

'What can I say?' I hoped I sounded suitably depressed. 'I could try pleading with you but that won't make you set me free.'

'You're right, of course.' Carl was clearly enjoying himself in his own petty sadistic way but I didn't mind. It was this same sadism which had made him overrule Steven. 'There's one thing I ought to explain, though. There aren't going to be any ships coming by to rescue you so I don't want you raising your hopes unnecessarily. I checked with the port authority in King's Lynn and there aren't any arrivals or departures scheduled until the evening tide tomorrow. You're still going to be aboard when the big bang comes.'

I did my best to look suitably cowed and disappointed. This was the way Carl wanted me to look and I've have hated to let him down. So long as I did as he expected he wouldn't start wondering what he'd done wrong.

'Well?' he enquired. 'Still keeping a stiff upper lip?'

I didn't bother to answer. Steven had started the outboard of the runabout and I wanted Carl to leave before he changed his mind about shooting me.

'It's time for me to be going, Philis,' Carl told me with a wolfish grin, 'but I should be hearing from you in a couple of hours. Have fun.'

Then he was gone, sliding the door closed behind him. It wasn't long before the sound of the outboard began to recede into the distance. I guessed it must be too cold and uncomfortable for Carl to sit around and gloat. Now it was up to me to ensure he didn't have anything to gloat about.

Harry Houdini wasn't the only man who knew how to slip out of a pair of handcuffs. It was one of the things I'd been taught on the SR(2) training course and I'd always been a quick learner in subjects which might help to save the precious Philis hide. Admittedly, I might have had problems if Carl or Steven had recognized their arse from their elbow and cuffed me properly. Fortunately they hadn't, any more than they'd thought to remove the contents of my pockets, and, using the special probe on my penknife, I was free of the table before the sound of the outboard had died away.

However, this early success wasn't any cause for complacency. Time-pencils were renowned for their lack of precision and, no matter what Carl had said about a couple of hours, I didn't like to think my life depended on how long the acid took to cut through the thin wire. I handled the device with the greatest respect, holding it at arm's length until I had it safely over the stern. Only then did I return to the galley to switch off the gas and open a couple of windows. It was a case of so far, so good. I was no longer going to help anybody prove or disprove the big bang theory but there was a long way to go before I was safe. I'd known all along that it was Carl's back-up plan which was most likely to kill me.

The first thing I did was go down below, and for once I found myself in total agreement with Carl – Steven really had done an excellent job on the bottom of the boat. There were three separate holes, and each of them was far too big for any hope of a temporary repair. As the tide came in, the front end of the cabin cruiser, which was still intact, would be eased clear of the sand, while more and more water flooded in through the holes at the stern; the weight of this sea-water would slide the boat backwards into the main channel, the current lending it a hand. A few minutes after that the cabin cruiser would sink like a stone.

For the moment, though, the boat was still wedged securely on the sandbank, and I had to make full use of this breathing space. It didn't take me very long to realize that there was very little hope of persuading anybody to come out into the estuary to rescue me. I knew the radio was out of commission, wrecked so thoroughly that there would have been no hope of repairing it even if I'd known how to do it. Even so, there should have been some other means of attracting attention. In all the books I'd ever read on the subject, sailors in distress always had rockets or Very pistols or smoke flares to guarantee their rescue. After I'd looked in the most likely places I decided I must have been reading the wrong kind of books, because I couldn't find a thing. Either Laura had had total confidence in her radio, or Carl and Steven had been more thorough than I'd anticipated.

There were, of course, other clever ways of signalling to the shore, and I was desperate enough to spare them a few seconds' consideration. It said a lot for my state of mind that I actually thought of trying to flash a message to the shore with the lounge lights. Fortunately it was only a momentary aberration, then a sense of reality returned. Even if the light of the hundred-watt bulb had been capable of carrying the several miles to shore, my life was too precious for me to gamble it on the outside chance that a Morse code expert would be gazing seawards at the appropriate moment. Setting fire to the *Laura* itself was a slightly better bet, but it smacked too much of lighting a funeral pyre. Although such a fire might well be noticed there was no saying how long it would be before anybody ventured out to discover the cause of the conflagration.

Rafts were out as well. I had neither the tools nor the time to construct a proper craft, and going into the sea with something which floated wasn't nearly good enough. To be any use to me the raft would have to float high enough to keep me clear of the water, and the choppy waves made this an impossibility. If I wanted to live, I'd have to go swimming, and I already knew where I intended to swim to.

However, as long as the boat stayed on the sandbank I'd no intention of even stepping out on deck. A strong wind was blowing up the Wash from the North Sea, driving short-lived but violent squalls of sleet along with it, and I had to keep both dry and warm for as long as possible. I also had to fortify the inner man in preparation for what lay ahead. Although there was no fresh food in the galley there was a fair selection of tinned food, and, after I'd closed the windows again, I put a couple of cans of oxtail soup on the stove to heat up, along with a tinned steak and kidney pudding. I might not be feeling particularly hungry, but my body was going to need as much food as I could force down.

While the food was cooking I went through the drawers and cupboards again, assembling a rudimentary survival kit. Its composition was largely determined by how much I could reasonably take with me. The two large polythene bags I'd found, presumably intended for refuse disposal, were the discovery which made such a kit feasible, and I didn't dare to use them separately. One bag would puncture more easily than a double thickness, and it was vital to try and keep what I took with me dry. The bottom of the sack was reserved for the oilskins I'd discovered stuffed in one of the lockers. On top of them went a couple of thick blankets, a pair of Laura's tights, and a chunky, cable-knit sweater which must have belonged to one of her sailor friends. A large pink bath towel went in as an afterthought, and then I couldn't afford any more bulky items. I had to reserve some room at the top for the clothes I was wearing.

170

When it came to selecting provisions, the unopened bottle of Dimple Haig was by far the most attractive item I came up with, but I rejected it on two counts. The most important of these wasn't that the whisky wouldn't do anything to improve my chances of survival. I simply couldn't risk the possibility of the bottle breaking inside the bag, because clothes soaked in whisky would be no better than clothes soaked in sea-water. While sardines and lump sugar weren't a particularly attractive alternative, they were the best I could do. I'd no way of knowing how long it would be before assistance arrived, so it was a case of any fuel being better than no fuel at all. Food equalled energy which meant heat, and my life was going to depend on how long I could survive in the sub-zero temperatures.

The same reasoning applied to the steak and kidney pudding. I knew people weren't advised to eat a heavy meal immediately prior to going for a swim, but I also knew they weren't advised to take a dip in the Wash on a freezing February night. It was a matter of endeavouring to balance evils, and this meant forcing the pudding down. Although it looked vile and tasted even worse, I persevered. I'd sent almost three-quarters of it down to join the soup before I received the signal that it was almost time for me to leave.

Yet again it had been a question of balance. If I'd left earlier, the tide wouldn't have risen so much. More of the sandbank would still have been above water, which meant I'd have been able to walk a few yards closer to the marker buoy I'd marked down as my refuge before I'd had to enter the water. Unfortunately, it would also have meant I'd have to spend longer clinging to the buoy. I'd compromised by deciding to hang on until the incoming tide had started to shift the stern of the grounded cruiser. The sudden movement of the deck beneath my feet told me the moment had arrived, and I began to undress.

By the time my clothes were in the bags and I'd smeared thick, black grease over my goose-pimpled body, I'd had plenty of opportunity to ask myself whether I was crazy or

171

not. When I considered the only possible alternatives, I knew I wasn't. The buoy, which looked to be about a quarter of a mile away, was my only chance with the boat sinking beneath me, and there was just the one way to reach it. I'd leave it to Navy men to go down with their ships.

Until I jumped off the *Laura* it hadn't even occurred to me that it might be possible to drown in sand. Carl and Steven must have taken the life-jackets when they'd removed the smoke flares and distress rockets, but they'd overlooked the solitary life-belt. I'd tossed it down on to the sandbank ahead of me, along with the carefully sealed bag, and I'd followed straight after them. It was only when I'd landed that I began to wish I'd paid more attention to what I was jumping into.

The first unpleasant shock had come when my feet had sunk into the sand instead of staying on the surface. The bow had been high enough for me to go in up to my knees when I'd landed, and the second even more unpleasant shock had come when I'd tried to free my legs. There was nothing for me to press my feet down against. Instead of stepping clear, I sank deeper into the clammy, semi-liquid sand. Worse than that, it actually seemed as though I was being sucked down. Thirty seconds of frenzied struggling, and I was embedded to my waist.

Although it wasn't easy to stop myself from being frenzied I managed it somehow, striving for a better distribution of my weight. I also tried to tread sand. This didn't stop me going down, but at least it slowed my descent sufficiently for me to take stock. The thing I regretted most of all, apart from having jumped into the quicksand in the first place, was throwing the life-belt quite so far. Although I hadn't consciously gone for distance it was well out of my reach, no matter how desperately I stretched. All the same, the life-belt had to be reached, and I could only think of one way to do it.

Throwing the top half of my body forward into the sand was one of the bravest things I ever wanted to do, and, it seemed, one of the least successful. The bottom half of my body was being gripped too tightly for it to be much of a dive, and I landed short. There were only a few inches between my outstretched fingers and the safety represented by the life-belt, but it might just as well have been miles, because it was impossible to swim in quicksand. I know, because I tried. The only discernible effect was that I sank faster than I would have done if I'd kept still.

Forty-five seconds had gone by now according to the stop-watch inside my head, and only my head and arms remained above the sand. I was drowning and I was freezing, and, until my fingers closed around the rope, I had no more than another thirty seconds before my nose and mouth were below the surface. The rope was attached to the life-belt, and I hauled it towards me, hand over hand. It didn't want to come, the quicksand clinging tenaciously to its prize, but it was a battle I couldn't afford to lose. Only when I had both of my hands gripping the cork did I take a rest.

I rested for all of two seconds, then I had to start fighting to save my life again because there was still an awful long way to go. The life-belt had enough buoyancy to save me from drowning, but it couldn't do anything to keep me warm, and, if it couldn't win one way, the sand was perfectly capable of freezing me to death. I was between the devil and the deep grey yuck. When I tried to use the buoyancy of the life-belt to pull myself free of the quicksand I discovered I'd have to think again. The side I pressed down on sank, while the opposite side rose into the air. Nor did I fare any better when I tried swimming again, pushing the life-belt ahead of me. Although the quicksand was thin enough to drown me, it was far too clinging for me to be able to kick my legs.

Almost two minutes had gone by now, and in another fif-teen I'd be too cold to hold on to the life-belt, let alone pull myself free. Nevertheless, I spared another half-minute or so for constructive thought. The infuriating thing was that I was only a yard or two from safety. The fire I'd started aboard the *Laura* before I'd abandoned ship was beginning to take a hold, and in the flickering light of the flames I could clearly see the bag I'd thrown on to the sand ahead of the life-belt. Although it wasn't nearly as heavy as me, the fact that it hadn't sunk at all suggested the sand must be considerably firmer.

While I knew what I had to do, I didn't relish letting go of the cork for even a second. On the other hand, I relished what would happen to me if I didn't even less. The first time I attempted the manoeuvre, I failed. There was a brief instant of utter panic as I realized my arms and shoulders were beneath the quicksand, and the sudden surge of adrenalin gave me the strength to wrench them free. At the second attempt I was more successful. I forced the life-belt upwards and towards me, then allowed it to drop over my head. Although the movement had the quicksand lapping at my chin, perilously close to my mouth, my arms were firmly anchored over the cork of the life-belt again.

It still wasn't easy. The life-belt could support the increased weight now I was in the middle of it, but the quicksand had the tenacity of fast-drying cement. I really had to battle for every inch of my body I freed, and the turning point didn't come until my waist had cleared the surface. After this it was only a few seconds before the rest of me was free and I was kneeling precariously on the life-belt, a life-belt which was slowly beginning to sink now all my weight was bearing down on it.

Unfortunately, kneeling wasn't quite good enough. I couldn't long-jump from my knees, and this was precisely what I had to do if I was going to reach ordinary slow sand. Even so, I never did manage to stand upright on the life-belt. I was no more than half-way to my feet when I felt my balance going, and I knew there weren't going to be any second chances on offer. If I did fall I'd be back in the quicksand again, and that would be an end to it. I wouldn't have the strength to free myself a second time. The best I could do was convert the fall into a jump, and pray this would carry me far enough.

There was a moment of almost exquisite delight when I felt

174

the soft sand pushing up as the top half of my body pushed down, but this wasn't a sensation I could afford to savour. The time for relief and self-congratulation would come when I was back on dry land, not when I was lying a few yards away from a potential bomb. By now, the strong wind had whipped the fire aboard the *Laura* into a raging inferno, and I shuddered to think how many gallons of fuel there must be aboard. Once I'd scooped up my survival kit I began to run, forcing my numbed limbs away from the boat, and gambling that there would be no more quicksand in my path. Of one thing I was positive. I might yet drown or die of exposure. I might even be run over by a supertanker or swallowed by a whale, but I was damned if I was going to be incinerated in the middle of the Wash by a fire I myself had started. That would have been too ridiculous for words.

There was no explosion. The same wind which had whipped up the flames must have also blown them away from the fuel tanks, and by the time I reached the far end of the sand-bar the flames had died down again. As I could barely distinguish the boat from a mere couple of hundred yards away, there was no chance at all of its being noticed on shore. If I managed to reach the buoy I'd have to reconcile myself to a long wait.

On the credit side, the run had helped to start my blood circulating again. Although I was still bitterly cold, burning up my body heat at an outrageous rate which I had no hope of replacing, I'd temporarily lost the dreadful chill I'd experienced while I'd been trapped in the quicksand. I'd encountered other areas of soft sand while I'd been running, some areas where I'd sunk in above my ankles, but there had been no more true quicksand. All that stood between me and my goal was another few hundred yards of rough arctic water.

I could remember reading an article which had said that the average human being could only survive for an hour in water whose temperature was one degree centigrade. It wasn't a statistic which did anything to comfort me. If everything went according to plan, I wouldn't be in the sea for

175

much more than ten minutes. However, in my particular situation there were other factors to be taken into account. I didn't have a thermometer with me, but the water in the Wash was certainly colder than one degree centigrade. Added to this, when I'd finished swimming I'd be facing another long stint of exposure, this time to the wind and sleet. Even if I managed to reach the cone-shaped buoy whose light I could see ahead of me my survival was going to lie in the lap of the gods. This was hardly a comforting thought to take into the water with me. Although I knew the buoy marked the main channel into King's Lynn, Carl had told me there wouldn't be any ships going in or out of the port for almost twenty-four hours. I had to pray that he was wrong.

At first, as I was temporarily out of the wind, the water almost seemed warm, but this was dangerously deceptive. Like the quicksand, the sea-water could freeze me to death as easily as it could drown. More dangerous still, the tide proved to be equally deceptive. In my rudimentary calculations I'd seen the incoming tide as an ally. It was going to sweep me right up to the buoy, saving me valuable calories and shortening the period I'd have to spend in the sea. As soon as I was in the water, in a position to appreciate just how powerful the current was, I realized my calculations had been wrong. There weren't going to be any free rides that night, and the only place the tide was sweeping me was straight past my target. The water was moving so fast it was going to take all my strength to work my way across the current to where I wanted to go.

In the end I was saved by the polythene bag containing my clothes and provisions. I'd anticipated it would be an encumbrance, looped over my right shoulder, and in one respect I was correct. With the bag pulling at me it was very difficult to maintain any kind of rhythm. Where I was lucky was that I'd automatically looped it over my right shoulder because this was where the marker-buoy was, over to my right. The drag of the bag, acting as a rudimentary sea anchor, could only have been marginal, but marginal influences were crucial. I was aiming for a few cubic feet of rusting metal in the middle of several square miles of estuary, and there were a few dreadful moments when I was certain I was going to miss. The tide was too strong, speeding along like a mill-race. It just wouldn't give me the time to make the last, vital few yards. Desperation did something to compensate, but it was the bag which saved me by banging into the buoy as I was swept past, swinging me around so I could grab a metal strut with one numbed, frozen hand. Although I knew the corroded metal must be doing terrible things to my flesh I was too cold to feel any pain. In any case, I didn't care. Now I'd reached the buoy, I could cross drowning off the list of ways I might die.

One of the biggest favours the bag had done me was to swing me around into the lee of the marker-buoy. As it wasn't a solid structure the water was still turbulent, but the Chinese-lantern shape broke up the waves and prevented the tide from buffeting me the way it would have done on the seaward side. Surprisingly, the part I'd been dreading most proved to be one of the easiest. Ever since I'd set out, a doubt had been nagging away at the back of my mind. There had always been the terrifying possibility that I might reach the buoy and discover there was no way of climbing up on to it. I'd had no means of knowing until I was close enough to distinguish a little more than the light on top.

As it turned out, there were no problems. Although I lost a lot more skin scrambling clear of the water, this seemed a very small price to pay. The real fun and games didn't start until I was safely on the buoy. Back on the boat my preparations had seemed logical enough. The key to my survival was going to be how successful I was in conserving body heat. It was going to be important to keep as dry as possible, which had seemed a very persuasive argument for bringing along a towel. Once I'd finished rubbing myself down, I'd pull on as many layers of clothing as possible, top off with the oilskins and then settle down to await deliverance, munching sardines and sugar lumps while I waited.

The basic logic still held true, especially now my naked, dripping body was once again exposed to the wind. Unfortunately, putting theory into practice became a waking nightmare when I was clinging to a bucking, unstable framework of rusted iron. Most of the time I needed two hands simply to hold on, and this didn't leave any spare for drying or dressing.

I never did get to dry myself, as a particularly strong gust of wind snatched the towel from my hand before I'd worked out how I was going to use it. In view of the sleet and driven spray I'd probably have been wasting my time, in any case. However, clothing was essential, and somehow or other I managed to pull on most of the garments I'd brought with me. It took me the best part of a quarter of an hour, and not all the clothes went on quite the way they were supposed to, but at least my body was protected.

It wasn't long before I began to suspect the whole operation had had as much value as sticking the feathers back on to a frozen turkey – the damage had already been done, and nothing was going to repair it. Sucking sugar lumps wasn't doing anything to make me any warmer, and I doubted whether the sardines would have done any better, even if I hadn't fumbled them back into the sea. My biggest regret concerned the bottle of Dimple Haig. While it might not have saved my life, at least I'd have been able to pass away happily.

CHAPTER XVIII

To begin with, when I first drifted back into consciousness, I thought I must still be on the marker-buoy. The gentle rocking motion was the same as it had been ever since the wind had dropped, and I could distinctly hear the slap of waves below me. I could also hear the sound of quiet voices.

Until I forced my salt-caked eyelids open I was positive I must be hallucinating, and even afterwards I wasn't entirely sure. The young man in the roll-neck sweater looked normal enough, but Mrs Robinson had assumed a new, surrealistic appearance.

'Your face is green,' I said accusingly, mumbling the words through cracked lips.

'I know,' she answered gruffly. 'I always have been a rotten sailor.'

She proved her point almost immediately. A larger wave hit the boat just as Mrs Robinson finished speaking, and she huddled over the blue plastic bowl she was clutching. Although she was heaving spectacularly enough she didn't appear to have a great deal left to bring up.

'How do you feel?' the man enquired.

'A hell of a sight warmer.' Somebody had stripped off my wet clothes, and I was cocooned on the bunk in several layers of blankets. 'What about Laura?'

'You mean Mrs Cunningham?'

Nodding my head was something I'd used to find easy. Now it was a real effort.

Fortunately, I didn't have anything else to do for the next few minutes except listen and continue the struggle to keep my eyes open. According to the man from Abercrombie's, Laura had been reasonably comfortable when they'd left her. The doctors, being doctors, had refused to commit themselves, but they seemed to think her head wound was only superficial, the bullet having glanced off her skull without penetrating. There certainly couldn't have been much wrong with her memory, because Laura was the one who had told Mrs Robinson of Elkhart's interest in her boat. If she hadn't, I'd still have been stuck in the middle of the Wash.

My greatest stroke of good fortune had been that Carl and Steven didn't know the first thing about head wounds. They'd been deceived both by the quantity of blood and the apparent position of the entry wound. It hadn't occurred to them to check Laura properly. I, on the other hand, had checked, and this had been one of the reasons I'd been in such a hurry to leave the cottage: Laura needed only to have come out with a single moan for Carl and Steven to finish off what Tuohy had started.

Mrs Robinson had been the other reason, and the instructions I'd left for her had been explicit. She was to ring Laura's cottage at nine o'clock precisely. If I didn't speak to her in person, and if I hadn't contacted her by ten, she was to gather reinforcements and head for Snettisham. I'd wanted to be long gone before she arrived. No matter how many reinforcements she brought with her, Carl and Steven would still have been the ones with the shotguns, and I hadn't wanted to be responsible for a full-scale massacre.

The man from Abercrombie's gave me one additional piece of information. According to what Laura had told Mrs Robinson, and in keeping with my own suspicions, it had been simple curiosity which had dragged her out to the farmhouse in the first place. What I'd told her about Elkhart and the Messengers had intrigued her, and a second-hand account hadn't been sufficient to satisfy her curiosity; she'd just had to see for herself. It hadn't occurred to her how pitifully thin any cover story would appear to Elkhart. Now she could regret her impulsiveness at leisure.

'What time is it?' I asked.

My eyelids were fighting to close, but I was holding them at bay for the moment.

'It's almost half past nine.'

'Morning or night?'

'Morning, of course.'

The man sounded surprised by my question. He'd no way of knowing I'd lost all track of time.

'This is important,' I said. 'I'm going back to sleep now, but I don't want you to take any action without consulting me. Don't do a thing until I'm awake again.'

Mrs Robinson raised her head from the bowl and started to say something. Unfortunately I was already sliding back into unconsciousness, and I couldn't muster the concentration to listen to her.

'Don't do a thing,' I mumbled. 'Not a thing.'

Then I was asleep.

As Denny would be footing the bill I had a private room at the hospital, but this wasn't enough to guarantee my privacy. The policeman leafing through a magazine in the chair beside my bed had the look of a permanent fixture. To begin with, he was too absorbed in his reading to notice my eyes were open. He had three stripes on his arm with which to justify this negligence. I was glad of the respite, because it gave me a few seconds to put my thoughts in order.

'I'm awake,' I announced once I was ready.

'I know,' the sergeant answered without raising his eyes from the page, 'but I'm not supposed to talk to you.'

He didn't, either, not a solitary word until the door of the room opened about twenty minutes later. The newcomer was in civilian clothes, but he obviously had rank. He only had to jerk his head for the sergeant to put down his magazine and leave.

'How do you feel?' he asked.

The policeman was careful to make sure I was aware of his indifference. This was considerably better than the active hostility I might have expected. SR(2) and the police were uneasy partners at the very best of times, and this definitely wasn't one of them.

'I'll live,' I told him.

'That's what all the doctors say, too. My name is Bluett, by the way. I've been detailed as liaison officer until our respective spheres of influence have been defined.'

His distaste came across as strongly as his indifference had done earlier.

'Lucky you,' I said. 'I assume you've already been in touch with London.'

'My superiors have been, yes. They've received their orders from above, so you'll be the one calling the shots.'

'That's nice.' Bluett's resentment made me grin. 'All you

181

have to do is make sure none of your lot rock the boat. The police keep their hands off unless I specifically tell you otherwise.'

As Bluett and I weren't destined to have a close working relationship, personal harmony wasn't of any great significance. It was far more important that he should have no doubts about the nature of such a relationship as we did enjoy.

'I see.' It was difficult to imagine how Bluett could have sounded less enthusiastic. 'All the same, I trust you will have the courtesy to keep me informed of any further developments.'

'My superiors will see to that, when, and if, it's necessary,' I agreed.

This wasn't much of an answer, and we both knew it. Pawson had been the one with the pull and the clout, and the access to high places. As a result, the police were being ordered to keep their noses out of something which was properly their business. It was a situation which understandably rankled, even at Bluett's lowly-individual level.

'There is one thing you could do for me, Mr Philis,' Bluett said, turning towards the door and speaking with controlled savagery. 'I'd be really grateful if you could try and keep an accurate body count for me. It will make it so much easier for me when I go along behind you to clear up the mess.'

I made no attempt to spoil his exit line. I reckoned Bluett deserved to land at least one good dig below the belt.

Despite Bluett's evident pessimism I wasn't anticipating any more bodies. While I wouldn't be backing off from trouble any more than I'd be offering guarantees of senior citizenship to Elkhart and company, my intentions were superficially peaceful. Everything had been brought out into the open now, the lines clearly delineated, and all that remained was to neatly wrap it all up. The manner in which I hoped to achieve this certainly wouldn't leave the police with any tidying up to do. Provided Elkhart saw sense there wouldn't be any more mess to clear up.

Even before I set out, I knew my arrival at the Messengers' headquarters was going to come as a big surprise to everybody. As was only to be expected, the media had all seized upon the sinking of the *Laura* and the shooting of its mistress with relish. It gave the newshounds some welcome relief from reporting blizzards, blocked roads and starving farm animals.

All the press releases had been carefully vetted by Pawson, and he'd orchestrated the whole press campaign to my specifications. The primary intention had been to bolster Elkhart's sense of security, and everything which had been released had been designed to have this effect. Although there were no outright lies there had been some distortions of the truth. Mrs Laura Cunningham, for example, was reported as being 'found shot at her cottage outside Snettisham.' Nowhere was there any suggestion that she might still be alive. In the same way, evidence for my own death was entirely negative. My name was never once mentioned in connection with the tragedy, and this was all the confirmation Elkhart would have required. There might not have been any mention of the explosion Carl and Steven would have told him to expect but the newspapers hadn't said a thing about anybody being rescued either. Elkhart would assume that the back-up plan had worked and I'd been drowned.

This was an assumption which began to lose its credibility when I was standing on the front doorstep of the farmhouse with Mrs Robinson beside me. She'd wanted to be in at the kill and I thought she'd more than earned the right, even if I hadn't taken her fully into my confidence. I'd no means of knowing how well-informed the girl who opened the door was, but she clearly recognized me. Her expression of welcome was the same as the one she'd have worn for the headless horseman or Count Dracula. I'd pushed past her before she'd decided whether she was going to scream or speak.

'Where's Elkhart?' I asked.

'The Reverend David, you mean? I don't know whether he's receiving visitors.'

'He'll want to receive me, love. It isn't every day he has an opportunity to talk with somebody who's walked in the Valley of Death.'

The girl was still dithering, unable to cope with a situation which went way beyond her previous experience, and Mrs Robinson wasn't prepared to wait for her to sort herself out. There was a large china pot containing some peacock feathers standing on a plinth just inside the front door. It was so ugly, decorated with a pseudo-classical Greek motif, that it deserved to be broken, and it made a most satisfactory noise when it hit the flagged floor. Mrs Robinson continued the good work with a few more of the breakables which were near to hand. By the time she'd cleared the first window-sill she'd assembled quite an audience, the disturbance attracting half a dozen of the harem from various parts of the house.

There was still no sign of Elkhart himself, but when Steven appeared, coming through the door which led to the back of the house, I signalled to her to abandon the senseless destruction. Although he was far enough away to have avoided me easily, the shock of seeing me had him temporarily rooted to the spot. By the time he'd decided he wanted to be somewhere else I was close enough to grab a handful of his sweater.

'Steven!' I exclaimed joyously, lifting him from his feet and swinging him around so he smacked into the wall. 'You're one of the people I wanted to see.'

I only had the chance to bounce him off the plaster a couple of times before Carl joined us, coming through the same door Steven had used. However, he'd had a few seconds longer to decide how he was going to react. Apart from the sound of breaking glass, one of the girls had screamed when I'd first laid hands on Steven, and this had been sufficient to make Carl bring his shotgun with him. I was sick and tired of seeing it in his hands every time we met, so I threw Steven at him before he could decide what he intended to do with it.

While the two of them were still untangling limbs, I retrieved the shotgun from the floor and tested its strength against the doorjamb. It disintegrated after the third swing, leaving me with the barrel in my hands while the stock skidded off across the floor. So did Carl after I'd hit him with the barrel, provoking a few more shrieks from the spectators. Carl's thoughts had probably been of escape, not aggression, when he'd pushed himself up from the floor, but any excuse would do. He didn't even twitch after a wall had stopped his further progress across the tiles. For a brief moment I wondered whether I might have hit him a little too hard, but I wasn't sufficiently bothered to check.

Steven didn't want to be hit, any more than he wanted to be shot when I showed him the gun I'd brought with me. He stayed down on the floor and looked frightened, which was very sensible of him. My memories of the nightmare in the middle of the Wash had suddenly come into very sharp focus, and it would have taken very little to provoke me into more violence.

'You can stand up now,' I told him, moving a couple of steps backwards in case close proximity tempted me. 'You have a little speech to make, explaining to the girls why you don't want them to telephone the police. If you want to avoid a charge of attempted murder, I'd be very convincing.'

Steven was far too frightened to be really eloquent, but he did his best. Not that it mattered either way, because I'd no intention of allowing anything to interfere with my conversation with Elkhart. It was something I'd been looking forward to.

One of the girls had warned Elkhart of our arrival, and he'd had plenty of time to compose himself. When Steven led us into his study we found him seated behind his desk, eyes closed, hands neatly folded in front of him. He didn't acknowledge our presence in any way, and I might conceivably have been impressed if I hadn't recognized Elkhart for the charlatan he was. However, he was a careful charlatan, as I discovered when I moved around behind him to check the drawers of his desk. The Beretta I removed from one of them could have been a reason for his apparent composure.

And it was only apparent, because when I looked closer the underlying tension was clearly visible. He was clenching his hands so tightly the knuckles showed white, and the tiny beads of perspiration which were forming on his forehead had no connection with the electric fire. Elkhart wasn't attempting to be defiant, he was simply trying to opt out, to avoid a confrontation he didn't know how to handle. His assumed meditation was a last resort, something he was trying because he didn't know what else to do.

After I'd made Steven lie down on the floor on his stomach and Mrs Robinson was comfortably installed in a chair by the door I added to Elkhart's tension by sticking the business end of the Beretta in his ear and clicking off the safety-catch. Although this didn't force Elkhart to open his eyes, it wasn't something he was prepared to suffer in silence.

'What do you want with me?'

His voice was trembling.

'Relax,' I told him. 'I've come here to reinforce your faith. I may not be able to walk on water, but I've definitely been resurrected.'

'I don't know what you're talking about. You're not making sense.'

By now Elkhart's eyes had opened. As the gun was still in his ear he couldn't move his head, but he was anxious to discover whether or not I intended to shoot him. The threat had served its purpose, and I moved away from Elkhart to sit in a chair to one side of his desk. This left me at a lower level than Elkhart, but I already had all the psychological advantage I needed.

'Come on, let's hear it all,' I said scornfully. 'Tell me you had no idea your two goons tried to kill me a couple of nights back.'

'You mean Carl and Steven?'

186

'They're the ones. They shipwrecked me on a sandbank in the middle of the Wash. My name wasn't mentioned but you must have read about it in the newspapers.'

'I don't believe it.' Although Elkhart wasn't at all convincing he was practising the line he intended to use at his trial. 'I don't know anything about it. Ask Steven if you don't believe me.'

'Well?' I enquired, kicking Steven none too gently on the ankle.

'It's true.' Steven sounded sullen and frightened, but he stuck to the official line. 'We didn't tell the Reverend David what we were doing, otherwise he would have stopped us. He didn't know anything about it.'

'And I suppose Tuohy was in Snettisham purely by chance.' Mrs Robinson was clearly enjoying herself and she'd no intention of being left out of the act. The big scene belonged to me but she was determined to get her twopenny worth in while she had the chance. 'If you're going to lie, you might at least try to be convincing. Would it make any difference to either of you to know Mrs Cunningham is alive and well? We were talking to her before we came here?'

I allowed the sudden silence to deepen while I lit myself a cigarette. Elkhart needed time to adjust his thinking to the implications of what Mrs Robinson had just told him.

'I'm no expert on the law,' I said, giving him a nudge in the right direction, 'but I'm sure the police could draw up quite an impressive list of charges.'

'Too true.' I could detect the relish in Mrs Robinson's gruff voice. 'Kidnapping, murder, rape. They can throw the book at you.'

'You said "could",' Elkhart had ignored Mrs Robinson and was grasping for the lifeline I'd thrown him. 'You mean to say you haven't been to the cops yet.'

'Not yet. I prefer to handle things my way.'

For a few dreadful seconds Elkhart was convinced I intended to shoot him there and then. I didn't immediately do anything to discourage this impression. I derived too much malicious enjoyment from watching Elkhart suffer.

'You're going to kill me?' he managed at last.

I smiled at him again and shook my head.

'For God's sake, what do you intend to do, then?'

For answer I reached into my jacket pocket and brought out the two typewritten sheets I'd brought with me. I threw them on to the desk in front of Elkhart.

'Read that,' I suggested. 'It should explain everything.'

Elkhart realized what I intended to do after the first two lines, but he read through to the end before he essayed a comment. His confidence was returning now he realized I had no physical violence on the agenda.

'You want me to send this to all the Messengers?'

'That's right,' I agreed. 'It will be your final Instruction, and it's the price you pay for freedom. The only alternative takes place in court and ends up with you spending a good few years of your life in prison. I'm leaving the choice to you.'

Elkhart nodded thoughtfully. Although he was taking his time about committing himself his mind was already made up. Indeed, I'd made the choice easy for him, because I'd deliberately been generous, far more generous than Elkhart had any right to expect. He'd probably attribute this to my ignorance about his financial affairs rather than to philanthropy. The truth was that there was nothing I could do about the five to ten million dollars Elkhart had salted away, according to the FBI, so I hadn't bothered to mention it. To Elkhart's way of thinking this should be more than sufficient to subsidize him in a comfortable retirement. However, he did have one objection to raise.

'I can already see a problem,' he informed me. 'My followers aren't going to believe this. They just won't accept it.'

'You're not going to allow them any alternative. I've only given you the framework for the Instruction. It's up to you to make it convincing. I'm sure a biblical scholar like you can find all manner of appropriate references to false prophets. The key sentence is where you tell your so-called disciples that you've been manipulating them, using their faith to lead them into the paths of ungodliness. Develop that theme and the message should be clear enough.'

The actual phrase I'd given Elkhart to build upon referred to 'leading you by your faith into the dark, Satanic labyrinths of my mind.' I'd thought this had a nice ring to it.

'It's really not going to be as easy as all that.' Elkhart wasn't deliberately creating obstacles. He'd already accepted that the Messengers would have to go if he wanted to stay out of prison. 'You're expecting me to destroy something that's taken years to build up.'

'You won't have to rely on the Instruction alone,' I told him. 'It will be confession time with the media as well. You're going on public record as the corrupt, perverted bastard we both know you to be. I shan't expect you to make any revelations which directly incriminate you, but I shall expect you to be very convincing. Otherwise Mrs Cunningham and I will be taking everything we know to the police.'

I only had to look at Elkhart's face to realize that this wasn't a prospect he relished. An Instruction was one thing, public self-abasement was quite another.

'If it's any help,' I went on, 'I'm giving you a time-table to work to. I'm allowing you exactly one week from today to wind up here in the UK and to be out of the country. After that you'll have another three weeks to dismantle your organization elsewhere. I'll be keeping a close watch on your progress, and I shan't be granting any period of grace. Either the Messengers are finished in a month, or you will be. I hope I've made myself perfectly clear.'

Once again Elkhart nodded his acceptance of my terms. There wasn't much else he could do in the circumstances, but he was no longer quite so convincing as he'd been before. The initial shock of my return from the grave had worn off, and there was no longer any threat to his person. It had encouraged him to start thinking of ways he might manage to wriggle off the hook, and this was an attitude I had to nip in the bud. The identity card I handed to Elkhart didn't mean a great deal to him, not even after he'd read it through twice, and he was clearly puzzled.

'What's this supposed to mean?' he asked.

'It's my way of showing you you're in far worse trouble than you'd imagined,' I explained. 'I'm not some private individual tilting at windmills. I have all the resources of an official government department behind me, and you can think yourself very fortunate that my superiors have chosen this way to deal with you. They don't mind you keeping your bank accounts in Switzerland, but they're not prepared to tolerate the Messengers any longer.'

My identity card should have told Elkhart a lot more than this. It demonstrated that there was no percentage in trying to arrange any more accidents for either Laura or myself, and once I'd made the point we left.

'You're very quiet,' I said to Mrs Robinson once we were outside the farmhouse. 'Don't tell me you've fallen under the Reverend David's spell.'

Her snort of derision showed exactly what she thought of my remark. This had been the first time Mrs Robinson had met Elkhart and he definitely hadn't been at his best.

'It's all the excitement.' She had a metaphorical tongue in her cheek. 'It's nice to see how the other half live but it was all a bit rich for my blood.'

'Come off it.' I didn't believe her for a moment. 'You loved every minute of it. I don't remember anybody asking you to start smashing up Elkhart's house.'

'I did enjoy that,' Mrs Robinson admitted, creasing her face into a smile. 'All the same, I was a little bit disappointed. I can't help thinking Elkhart has escaped far too lightly. Even if he does disband the Messengers, he's still getting away with murder.'

'Don't you believe it,' I told her. 'Keep an eye on the newspaper headlines. You'll find out he isn't going to get away with a thing.'

I had as strong a sense of justice as Mrs Robinson. What she didn't know was that the arrangement she'd just witnessed was merely the window-dressing, the icing on top of the cake. Although I'd every intention of keeping to my side of the bargain with Elkhart, Simon Denny hadn't been a party to it. We'd had our discussion about Elkhart's fate the previous night.

To begin with, Denny hadn't been at all enthusiastic. I'd started by giving him what he'd paid me for, an explanation for his daughter's murder. There were one or two small gaps in the story where I had to rely on guess-work, but Brown had given me enough for me to be able to construct a fairly detailed account of how and why Vanessa had died. Although Denny had listened to me in silence without any interruptions, I'd been aware of his mounting anger, his sense of outrage at what had happened to his only daughter. When I'd finished, I'd shown Denny my rough draft for Elkhart's final Instruction. Denny had responded by virtually throwing it back in my face.

'It's not enough, Philis,' he'd almost shouted, his whole face contorted by a mixture of grief and anger. 'Not nearly enough. Elkhart would escape scot-free.'

'So what's the alternative?' I asked. 'Do you really want to take him to court?'

I'd deliberately emphasized my scepticism.

'Why not? We have enough to convict him, don't we?'

'More than enough if that's really what you want to do.'

I already knew what I wanted to do, and I wasn't going to win Denny over by laying all my cards on the table at the same time. This was why I elected not to say any more. I sipped my whisky instead, watching Denny over the rim of my glass. It was only a few seconds before his brain had resumed full control again, and this was the point where he realized I must have more to offer.

'OK, Philis,' he said, going across to refill his glass. 'Let's start again. Perhaps you'd like to explain why you're opposed to allowing the law to take its course.'

I went through the points one by one, ticking them off on my fingers. My own chief objection was that I'd be expected

191

to appear in court to present my evidence. This would necessarily give rise to any number of problems, both for myself and for the department. Worst of all, the resultant publicity could well destroy any value I had as a field operative, and, however much I might complain to Pawson, I didn't want to spend the rest of my working life chained to a desk. I just didn't have the temperament for it.

Although Denny appreciated my dilemma, and was suitably understanding, my second point carried far more weight with him. Vanessa might be dead, but her memory was still dear to Denny, as was her mother's. If we went the whole hog and tried for the murder conviction Elkhart so richly deserved, his defence attorneys would be spending a great deal of time concentrating on the private details of the Denny family's life. A lot of old wounds, and some new ones, would inevitably be opened and left to fester. Vanessa herself was hardly likely to be portrayed in a sympathetic light.

However, the argument which finally won Denny over concerned Elkhart himself. If he was brought to trial, he'd certainly be convicted of something. There could be no possible doubt about this. At the very least he'd be sentenced to several years in prison. Unfortunately, by bringing him to trial we'd be running the very real risk of turning Elkhart into a martyr in the eyes of his followers. The Messengers were fanatics of a kind, and fanatics weren't usually impressed by evidence given in court. If we allowed the organization to remain intact the Messengers would almost certainly assume society was persecuting their leader in the same way Jesus had been persecuted before him. Worse still, there was the danger somebody else might take over the Messengers, keeping the sect alive and acting as caretaker until Elkhart was free to resume control again. An added danger was that the publicity attending the trial might even bring new converts flocking to the Messengers.

'All right, Philis,' Denny conceded. 'You've made your point, but this still isn't enough.' He was indicating the proposed Instruction. 'I've lived among the Arabs for too many years not to have picked up some of their attitudes. Elkhart and his minions murdered my daughter. I want vengeance.'

'Would this help?'

I'd had the piece of paper ready in my hand for the last few minutes. Now I handed it across to Denny and allowed him to read the three names and addresses which were written on it.

'What is this?' he asked uncomprehendingly.

It didn't take me very long to explain. As I pointed out to Denny, there were plenty of Tuohys around, people who were prepared to kill provided they were paid for their work.

'You have plenty of money,' I told him. 'If you choose to spend some of it on any of the men listed there, you'll find they're both reliable and discreet. All I ask is that you allow Elkhart a month to disband the Messengers. Then you're at perfect liberty to do what you want.'

Although Denny didn't immediately commit himself, the expression on his face left very little room for doubt. It was the outward manifestation of an attitude Elkhart himself should have appreciated. After all, an eye for an eye was one of his favourite biblical themes.

ABOUT THE AUTHOR

Ritchie Perry was born in King's Lynn, England, and educated at St. John's College, Oxford. He currently resides in Bedfordshire, where he is a primary school teacher.

Other books in the Philis–Pawson series by Ritchie Perry include: *The Fall Guy, A Hard Man to Kill, Ticket to Ride, Holiday with a Vengeance, Your Money and Your Wife, One Good Death Deserves Another,* and *Bishop's Pawn.*